Daisy ignored the red flag that warned against spending too much time with the wickedly charming Luiz Valquez. She had asked for four days and now she had the chance to have four weeks. She'd wanted a walk on the wild side, hadn't she? This was her chance to make it one to remember.

'OK. You're on.'

Luiz took her by the shoulders and pressed a blisteringly hot kiss to her mouth. Daisy leaned into him, unable to help herself from responding with burgeoning passion. He only had to touch her and she erupted into flames. She could feel the heat rushing through her veins, sending electric sensations through every cell in her body.

His hands cupped her face, his fingers splaying out over her cheeks as he deepened the kiss. His tongue played cat and mouse with hers, teasing and taunting hers to fight back. She flicked her tongue against his, doing her own little teasing routine, delighting in the way he groaned in the back of his throat and brought his pelvis hard against hers. She felt the hard ridge of him, the pressure of his blood building as his desire for her escalated.

'Relax for me, *querida*,' he whispered against the skin of her neck.

THE PLAYBOYS OF ARGENTINA

Introducing the untameable Valquez brothers...

The Valquez brothers are living legends.

Alejandro's business prowess is staggering,
Luiz's success on the polo field is unparalleled,
and their reputations in the bedroom are scandalous!

But they're both about to face their biggest challenge yet…

Alejandro must marry—
but he never anticipated desiring his convenient wife!

And notorious playboy Luiz finds his match
in the delectably innocent Daisy Wyndham!

You won't want to miss this scorching new duet
from Melanie Milburne!

You read Alejandro's story in:
THE VALQUEZ BRIDE
October 2014

Now read Luiz's story in:
THE VALQUEZ SEDUCTION
November 2014

THE VALQUEZ SEDUCTION

BY

MELANIE MILBURNE

Published in Great Britain 2014
by Mills & Boon, an imprint of Harlequin (UK) Limited,
Eton House, 18-24 Paradise Road, Richmond, Surrey, TW9 1SR

ISBN: 978-0-263-24323-9

Harlequin (UK) Limited's policy is to use papers that are natural, renewable and recyclable products and made from wood grown in sustainable forests. The logging and manufacturing processes conform to the legal environmental regulations of the country of origin.

Printed and bound in Great Britain
by CPI Antony Rowe, Chippenham, Wiltshire

From as soon as **Melanie Milburne** could pick up a pen she knew she wanted to write. It was when she picked up her first Mills & Boon® at seventeen that she realised she wanted to write romance. Distracted for a few years by meeting marrying her own handsome hero, surgeon husband Steve, and having two boys, plus completing a Masters of Education and becoming a nationally ranked athlete (masters swimming), she decided to write. Five submissions later she sold her first book and is now a multi-published, bestselling, award-winning *USA TODAY* author. In 2008 she won the Australian Readers' Association most popular category/series romance and in 2011 she won the prestigious Romance Writers of Australia R*BY award.

Melanie loves to hear from her readers via her website, www.melaniemilburne.com.au, or on Facebook: www.facebook.com/pages/Melanie-Milburne/351594482609

Recent titles by the same author:

THE VALQUEZ BRIDE
(The Playboys of Argentina)
AT NO MAN'S COMMAND
PLAYBOY'S LESSON
(The Chatsfield)
NEVER GAMBLE WITH A CAFFARELLI
(Those Scandalous Caffarellis)

CHAPTER ONE

IT ONLY TOOK Daisy Wyndham three and a half blocks to shake off her father's bodyguard. She grinned as she joined her two teaching friends inside the Las Vegas hot spot nightclub where they planned to kick off their half-term holiday before the winter school term in London resumed. 'See?' She high-fived Belinda and then Kate. 'I told you I'd make it before the first round of drinks. That's a new record too. It usually takes me at least five blocks to lose Bruno when I'm abroad.'

Kate, recently appointed to teach Year Three, handed her a glass of champagne with a frown pleating her brow. 'Is this going to happen *every* night we're here on holiday?'

Belinda from Grade Four rolled her eyes. 'I did warn you, Kate. Travelling abroad with Daze means excess baggage in the shape of a big hairy scary guy carrying a concealed weapon. Get used to it. It ain't going to change any time soon.'

'Oh, yes it is.' Daisy set her posture in a determined line. 'I'm sick of being treated like a little kid. I'm plenty old enough to take care of myself. And this holiday is the perfect chance to prove it.'

Once and for all.

Her father would have to get over it. She wanted to live her life the way she wanted to live it. Not be answerable to her dad, who thought she was still twelve years old.

'Why's your dad so protective anyway?' Kate asked.

Daisy took a sip of her drink before she answered. She hadn't told anyone of her father's former and thankfully brief connection with the underworld. It was far easier to pretend he was overly protective because she once went missing for half an hour as a child. That her disappearance had been nothing more than a case of her hiding from her mother behind a rack of dresses in Marks and Spencer was beside the point. 'My dad watches too many scary movies. He thinks as soon as I step foot in a foreign country someone is going to kidnap me and demand a ransom.'

Kate raised her brows. 'I realised you came from money but—'

'Pots and pots of money.' Belinda held her glass out for a refill. 'You should see her dad's estate in Surrey. Massive. He has villas in Italy and the South of France too. I didn't realise being an accountant could be so lucrative. Maybe I should've done that instead of teaching.'

Daisy chewed the edge of her lower lip. She had always believed her father's wealth was gained through hard work and discipline, building up his London accounting firm from scratch. She *still* believed it…sort of. How could she believe anything else? He was a loving dad who consecrated the ground she walked on. So what if he had once done a teensy weensy accounting job for a Mafia boss? That didn't make *him* a criminal. He had assured her it had been years and years ago and there was no reason to be worried now, although why he insisted she have top level security at her flat and always travel abroad with a bodyguard did make her feel a smidgeon of disquiet if she were to be perfectly honest. But that was something she had always put up with because it was easier than arguing with him about it. Arguing with her father was an exhausting and pointless exercise, which her mother, Rose, had found out the hard way when she'd tried to divorce him.

'If you've got so much family money why bother teaching?' Kate asked.

'I love teaching,' Daisy said, thinking of her kindergarten class with their sunny and earnest little faces. 'The kids are so innocent and—'

Belinda gave a half snort, half laugh as she wiped up a dribble of bubbles off the side of her glass with her fingertip. 'Yeah, like you.'

Daisy sent her a mock glower. 'Just because I'm technically still a virgin doesn't mean—'

'Technically?' Kate frowned in puzzlement. 'What? You mean you haven't actually *slept* with a guy?'

Here we go, Daisy silently groaned. Why was being a virgin such an oddity these days? Plenty of girls didn't sleep around. What about Amish girls? Or girls from other religious persuasions? Nuns, for instance. Anyway, having an overprotective father was like being raised in a convent. He'd practically strip-searched every suitor she'd ever had. He did background checks on them too. It was beyond embarrassing. Which was how she had ended up twenty-six years old without having done the deed.

But this holiday was going to change all that. Or so she hoped. Away from her father's watchful eye, she would be able to stretch her dating wings. Flirt a little. Relax instead of being uptight about the whole process in case her father suddenly appeared, waving a warrant for her date's arrest.

'Not yet,' Daisy said. 'But I'm not going to do it just for the sake of it. I want it to mean something. I want it to mean something for the guy too.'

'I hate to be the one to tell you this but you're unlikely to find your soulmate in Vegas,' Kate said.

'Don't feel too sorry for her,' Belinda said with a naughty grin. 'Our Daze has a toy. I gave it to her when we did Secret Santa with the staff at school last year. Didn't I, Daze?'

Daisy laughed it off but she hated that she still blushed over that wretched sex toy. She'd only taken it out of the box a few times… OK, well, maybe more than a few times. Truth be told, she hadn't put it *back* in the box. It was currently in her make-up bag in her hotel room because she hadn't wanted her new nosy flatmate to find it in her bedside drawer while she was away. Anyway, it had an absolutely brilliant massage attachment that was really handy when her neck or shoulders got tense.

'Hey, check out two o'clock.' Belinda jerked her head

towards the right hand end of the bar. 'The guy standing next to the girl in the dress that looks like aluminium foil. Do you know who it is?'

Daisy studied the tall black-haired man leaning indolently against the bar as he chatted to a young woman dressed in a tight sheath of a shimmering dress that clung to every curve of her supermodel-perfect body. The man's open-necked shirt was startlingly white against his deep tan and his eyes were so dark they looked as black as molasses. His hair was long enough to curl against his collar and was tousled, as if he'd not long tumbled out of bed or run his hands through it, or both. His mouth was nothing short of mesmerising. A sculptured sensual curve surrounded by a day or two of dense black stubble, the top lip curved upwards in a smile that looked more cynical than amused, and a bottom lip that hinted at a dangerously healthy sexual appetite. In spite of the heat in the crowded nightclub Daisy felt an involuntary shiver run over her flesh. 'No, who is it?'

'Luiz Valquez,' Belinda said. 'He's a famous Argentinian champion polo player. He's nicknamed in the press as the king of one-night stands. There's not a playboy out there who can change partners as fast as he does. He's practically turned it into a sport. Talk about smoking-hot.'

Hot wasn't even close, Daisy thought. She hadn't seen a man who looked anywhere near as heart-stoppingly handsome as him. He looked like one of those male magazine models, the ones who advertised designer eyewear or expensive aftershave. Oozing testosterone and sex appeal. Simmering with sensual energy that radiated out from him in soundless waves. She couldn't seem to drag her gaze back to her friends. It was glued to the man as if invisible wires had tethered her eyeballs. There was something about him that was so...hypnotic. Captivating. It wasn't just his staggeringly gorgeous good looks. There was something about his aura of supreme confidence she found intensely intriguing. She could see it in the arrogant tilt of his head, the hawk-like blade of his nose, the sharply intelligent gaze. It was as if he knew he was in command of the room and was biding his time to demonstrate it.

'Stop drooling, Daze,' Belinda said. 'He doesn't associate with mere mortals like us. He only ever dates supermodels or Hollywood starlets.'

Daisy was about to look away when he suddenly turned his head and his dark-as-night eyes met hers across the crowded nightclub. An electric jolt shot through her as his black brows lifted in blatant male appraisal. A hot spurting sensation arrowed between her legs and she almost fell off the bar stool she was perched on. She quickly crossed her legs but his gaze followed her right thigh as it hooked over her left one. Then his gaze came up ever so lazily the whole length of her body from ankle to hip, from her waist to her breasts, stalled there for a pulse-thundering pause, before coming up to her mouth.

He paused again. Longer this time.

Daisy felt her lips burn as if he had pressed a hot brand to them via his sexily hooded gaze. He then moved his gaze from her mouth to do a leisurely sweep of her chestnut hair, which she had bundled into a half-up, half-down do that framed her face and brushed her shoulders at the same time.

Then he came back to her eyes.

Daisy had heard the expression 'time stood still' many times. She had even used it on occasion. She knew it wasn't logically possible but this time it really *did* stop. She felt it. It was as if every clock in the night-club, every clock on every smartphone, every watch on every wrist shuddered and then stopped.

Tick. Tock. Stop.

Belinda snapped her fingers in front of Daisy's face. 'Earth to Daze.'

'Oh, my God.' Kate nudged Daisy in the ribs. 'He's coming over!'

Daisy sat with her heart pounding like a piston in an engine long overdue for a service. Her skin felt tin-gly all over. She could even feel the backs of her knees fizzing like sherbet trickled into a glass of soda. She felt giddy. She had to grip the edge of the bar with one of her hands to stop from tumbling to the floor in an ungainly heap.

She couldn't remember a time when a man had looked at her like…like *that*. As if she was the only woman in the room. As if he could see through her little black dress to the black bra and lacy knickers she was wearing underneath. As if he could see how her body was responding to him of its own volition, as if he had cast some kind of magic spell over her. It was shock-ing and yet somehow wickedly thrilling to feel as if she had no control over her body or her senses. It was as if the universe had heard a whisper of her desire to step out of her good girl shoes and was offering her up the most tempting bad boy man on the planet. No man had ever singled her out in such a brazenly sexual way. No man had ever triggered such a primal need in her. It pumped through her body like a potent steroid, making her aware of every inch of her flesh.

As he walked across the dance floor Daisy was reminded of Moses parting the Red Sea. Not that this particular Moses would be taking any notice of the Ten Commandments, she thought wryly. He had probably broken every one of them before breakfast. She watched as people stepped back in unison like a standing Mexican wave, and even the strobe lighting seemed to highlight his progress as if his coming over to speak to her was the main event of the evening.

He came and stood in front of her, so close her crossed over right knee was almost touching his trouser zip. Her kneecap began to twitch, the nerves beneath the skin doing frantic little somersaults at the thought of brushing against that hard and potent male body.

His mouth curved upwards in a smile so arrantly sexy it should have had an Adults Only rating. '*Hola*.'

Daisy practically melted into a pool of molten wax at his feet when she heard his deep baritone voice greet her in his native tongue. Spanish was delightful to hear from just about anyone's mouth but never more so than from an Argentinian's. The influences on Argentina from large migrations of Italians in the nineteenth century gave the accent in some regions an Italian flair that was as lyrical as music. But reading such information in a travel guide hadn't prepared her for the real thing.

She sat spellbound and speechless for five full seconds as the sound of his voice moved its way through her body like a seductive caress. She felt a slow blush creep over her cheeks and finally managed to get her voice to come out of her throat. It was a little mortifying it came out like a mouse squeak, but still… 'Hi… erm…hello.'

Luiz Valquez's eyes were even darker up close. She couldn't find his pupils in that glinting sea of bottomless black. His mouth was even more tempting now she could see its contours so intimately. His philtrum running down from beneath his nose was so well defined she could have placed her pinkie fingertip in the dish between the stubble-coated lines. She curled her fingers into her hand to stop from actually doing so. The force field of his body was so strong she felt like a microscopic iron filing in front of an industrial strength magnet. Pull. Pull. Pull. It was all she could do to remain upright on the bar stool.

'Would you like to dance?' He asked the question in English but with that distinctive accent wrapped around every word it made her spine feel as if someone was unbolting each vertebra.

But the confidence and self-assurance she had admired just a moment before now began to annoy her. He *expected* her to say yes. Kate and Belinda expected her to say yes. The whole nightclub crowd expected her to say yes.

Physically she wanted to say yes, but her rational

mind snapped back to attention like a soldier clicking his heels in front of a drill sergeant. The one thing she loathed in a potential date was cocksure arrogance. Who the hell did he think he was? He could go and crook his little finger someplace else. If and when she got involved with someone it would be with someone who had the decency to treat her as an equal, not like some desperate little sports star groupie looking for a quick trophy shag.

'No.' Daisy softened it with a brief smile that didn't show her teeth. 'Thanks anyway.'

Something in his pitch-black eyes sharpened. His nostrils widened as if taking up the challenge of getting her to change her mind privately excited him. His charming smile, however, didn't falter. 'You're with someone?'

'No...I mean yes. My friends from school. The school I teach at. *We* teach at. In London.' Daisy pointed at her friends, only to find they weren't there. They had slipped off the bar stools next to hers and were currently dancing on the dance floor with two men she'd seen them chatting to as she'd come in from shaking off her bodyguard.

Thanks a bunch, girls.

He followed the line of her gaze. 'They look like they're having fun.'

What did he mean? That she wasn't? That she was too strait-laced and uptight to have a good time? She might not be used to colouring outside the lines but she had her crayons sharpened. But she was going to use them on someone a little less self-assured than him. 'Yes, they are.' Her chin went up. 'So am I.'

The meshing of his brown-black gaze with her blue one felt like a taser shock to her system. Her whole body reacted with a zinging fizz that whizzed through her blood like a missile. 'Is this your first time?'

Daisy felt her blush spread a little further until her whole body felt as if it was being engulfed by fire. How could he know that? How could he possibly know *that*? 'Erm…in Vegas, you mean?'

His slow smile tilted the side of his mouth. It tilted her stomach as well, like a paper boat on a tidal wave. '*Sí*.'

Oh, God, please don't keep speaking in Spanish or I will sleep with you. Here. On the floor right in front of everyone. 'It's my first time to the US, and yes, to Vegas as well.'

'What do you think of it so far?'

Daisy kept her gaze locked on his, not that she had any choice in the matter. Her eyes weren't responding to the message from her brain to stop staring at him like a star-struck fan in front of a Hollywood superstar. 'It's bold and brash and in-your-face. Vegas, I mean. Not the States in general. I haven't been anywhere else except LA and that was only when we landed at the airport.'

'Did you fly or drive down?'

'We came by bus.'

His half smile was still doing weird and exciting things to her insides. His smell was doing equally weird and exciting things to her senses. His citrus-based cologne had grace notes of a rain-washed cypress pine forest that was powerfully intoxicating. For a tiny moment Daisy wondered if she'd done the wrong thing in knocking back his offer of a dance. She was supposed to be fluttering her flirting wings. What better way to get off the ground than with a bad boy who did nothing but flirt and have fun? But then she saw the anticipatory glint in his eyes. He thought he had her in the bag—erm, bed. *Damn him.*

'How long are you staying in Vegas?' he asked.

'Four days.'

His eyes moved over her face again, as if memorising her features. He lingered a little too long on her mouth, making her itch to send out her tongue to moisten her lips. Daisy had never been more conscious of her body language. She knew it had the potential to contradict every word she said. If it hadn't already.

'If you change your mind about that dance I'll be over there.' He jerked his head towards the area of the bar he had come from.

She raised her chin again, giving him a pointed look. 'With your date?'

He gave a negligent shrug of one of his broad shoulders. 'She's someone I just met.'

'And will sleep with just the once before you move on to the next candidate?'

His smile widened. 'You've heard about me?'

Daisy gave him the sort of look she would give one of the naughtiest boys in her kindergarten class. 'It's not a reputation to be proud of. Sleeping your way around the world with a bunch of nameless women you'll never see again.'

His eyes glinted wickedly. 'It's a tough gig but someone's got to have the stamina to do it.'

Do it. The words triggered a flood of erotic thoughts to her mind. Him doing it. Her doing it. *With him.* Their naked bodies wrapped together, his hair-roughened thighs entrapping hers, his hands cupping her breasts, touching her in that secret valley between her thighs.

Daisy suppressed a whole body shudder, somehow keeping her features in her best haughty schoolmistress mask. But, looking at his dancing black eyes, she suspected he knew exactly the effect he was having on her. It was the same effect he had on any woman with a pulse. He was utterly gorgeous. Über-sexy. Terrifyingly irresistible.

She gave him another one of her stiff on-off smiles to disguise the torment of temptation currently assailing her. 'Will you excuse me? I'm falling behind my friends in the having-a-good-time stakes.'

He didn't move a millimetre, which meant she had to sidle down off the stool and brush past his tall muscle-packed frame. The shock of his body against hers was like coming into contact with an electric fence. She glanced up at the laughing gleam of his gaze and another fiery blush swept over her entire body.

'A word of advice before you go.'

Daisy pursed her lips. 'Go on.' *If you must.* She didn't say that bit out loud. She didn't need to. Her folded arms and rolled eyes said it for her.

He pointed to the drink she had left behind. 'Don't leave your drinks unattended.'

She gave him an irritated glance. How galling to

have him point out her oversight. It made her feel all the more foolish and gauche. 'I *have* been out at night before.'

'Maybe, but some of the nightclubs along the strip have had a problem with drink spiking. Better to be safe than sorry.'

'I know how to take care of myself.'

His eyes had the most annoying habit of staring at her mouth, which made her want to stare at his. She fought the impulse but within a heartbeat her gaze had tracked to the sensual seam that was no longer smiling but set in more serious lines. For some reason it made him even more stop-the-traffic gorgeous. She drew in a breath that felt as if it had thumbtacks attached. The ear-throbbing music faded into the background. The sweaty, gyrating crowd on the dance floor might have been in another state for all the notice she took of them. In spite of all the competing aftershaves and expensive perfumes, she could still smell him. The sharp fresh tang of his cologne was imprinted in her brain and she knew she would never be able to walk past a cypress pine without wanting to hug it. It was a shame he was so arrogant. A little fling with someone like him would have been fun to talk about with the girls when she got home.

But a one-night stand?

Out of the question.

Daisy gave him an arch look. 'Do I have lipstick on my teeth or something?'

'Why don't you smile so I can check?'

She pressed her lips together. *Where was a naughty*

step when you needed one? 'Why did you come over to talk to me?'

His eyes twinkled as they held hers. 'I saw you staring at me.'

'I wasn't staring!' Daisy spluttered. 'My friends pointed you out and I merely glanced at you to see if I recognised you, which I didn't. Sorry if that upsets your ego.' She wasn't one bit sorry.

A hint of a smile still lurked in the black ink of his eyes. 'It doesn't.'

'No, I imagine not.' She knew she sounded ridiculously prim but she couldn't seem to help it. The words kept coming out in a steady stream—sounding scarily like Miss Edith Cassidy, her starchy soon-to-retire headmistress. 'I expect you're used to young women the world over dropping into a swoon when they see you but I'm not one to be impressed by outward appearances.'

'What does impress you?'

Daisy paused as she thought about it. 'Erm…'

He leaned back against the bar and crossed one ankle over the other as if prepared to settle in for the night. 'Money?'

She frowned. 'Of course not.'

His mouth curved in a cynical arc. 'What, then?'

'Manners. Intellect. Morality.'

His smile became an amused chuckle. 'An old-fashioned girl hanging out in Vegas. Who would've thought?'

Daisy was sure she would have permanent lines around her mouth from all the lip-pursing she was doing. 'Were you born naturally obnoxious or is it something you've worked on over the years?'

He pushed himself away from the bar and ran an idle fingertip down the length of her bare arm from her shoulder to her wrist, still with that mocking smile curving his mouth. 'Save the last dance for me, *querida*.'

Daisy gave him a withering look as she brushed past him to join her friends, 'Dream on.'

Luiz decided to leave the nightclub at 3:00 a.m. He'd lost sight of the English girl when he'd stopped to chat to someone he knew on the polo circuit. By the time he'd turned around again she had disappeared. He refused to acknowledge the strange little pit of disappointment in his belly. Easy come, easy go. There were plenty of other girls he could pick up if he could be bothered.

He wasn't sure what it was about her that fascinated him so much. She wasn't his usual type with her girl-next-door looks and prim goody-two-shoes manner. But her chestnut hair had highlights that shone like spun gold and her darkly lashed intensely blue eyes reminded him of the Aegean Sea. Her skin had that roses and cream bloom young English women were famous for and her mouth was generous and full, suggesting a passionate nature behind the haughty I'm-too-good-for-the-likes-of-you air she affected.

He'd spent most of the evening watching her watching him. It amused him to see her try and disguise her interest. Hiding behind a drink she barely touched or the shoulder of one of her friends. Pretending to be having a good time when clearly the nightclub scene was not her usual stomping ground. For all that she'd dressed for the part in a little black dress and high heels, she looked out of place. She reminded him of Bambi pretending to be Barbarella.

Luiz walked back to his hotel room alone. He'd had plenty of offers he could have taken up but for once he wasn't in the mood. He was still shaking off the jet lag from when he'd flown in from Argentina, where he'd spent some time with his older brother and his new wife, Teddy. Seeing his brother so happy had triggered a restless feeling he couldn't block out with endless partying. It used to be just him and Alejandro. They were a team. The playboy Valquez brothers, notorious the world over for having a good time. Women flocked to them wherever they went.

Now Luiz was on his own, wandering around the globe in search of the next victory on the polo field. Trophy after trophy lined the bookshelves at his villa—the villa he only ever visited when the polo schedule allowed. He lived out of an overnight bag; he didn't stay long enough in one place to warrant a suitcase. He checked in and checked out of hotels like he checked in and out of relationships. One-night stands were his speciality. What was the point of hanging around for someone to do the check out on you? He had seen his mother do that to his father. He had seen his brother suffer the public humiliation of being jilted at the altar ten years ago. Sure, Alejandro was happy now, and Teddy seemed like a top sort of girl, but that sort of commitment wasn't for him.

No one was *ever* going to have the power to hurt him. Again.

Luiz was five doors away from his suite when he saw her—the English girl with the cut-glass accent. She was with a man who was leading her by the hand towards a room on the other side further down the corridor. However, something about the little tableau didn't seem right. The English girl was not steady on her feet and her blue eyes were no longer clear and bright but glazed and disoriented.

'What are you looking at?' the man with her snarled at Luiz.

Luiz glanced at the English girl. 'Are you all right, *querida*?'

The girl looked at him vacantly, her head lolling to one side. 'I need to go to bed…'

'In here, sugar,' the man said as he shouldered open his door.

Luiz put his arm across the door jamb like a blockade. 'You want me to call the cops or will you let her go quietly?'

The man breathed alcohol fumes over Luiz's face. 'She wants to be with me. She said so earlier.'

Luiz wanted to punch the man's teeth into the back of his preppy pretty boy head. 'She's not capable of saying anything and you damn well know it. Did you do this to her? Give her something in her drink to make her come with you?'

The man gave him a *cool it* look. 'Hey, man, what's your problem? Is she yours or something?'

Luiz felt a sour taste come up in his mouth. Anger came

up with it, moving through his body like a bloated tide. What sort of man treated a woman like a toy they could pick up off a shelf? *You do*, a little voice piped up. He brushed aside the pricking arrow of his conscience and directed his ire where it belonged right now. 'I'm going to ask you again. Did you do this to her?'

The man's eyes darted either side of the corridor. 'Is this a sting or something? Are you undercover?'

Luiz grabbed the man by the throat and pushed him back against the wall so hard all the pictures hanging along the corridor rattled in their frames. 'I'm going to give you three minutes to check out of this hotel. After that I'm calling the cops. Got it?'

The man swallowed against the heel of Luiz's hand. 'I didn't do it. It was my mate. He said it wouldn't hurt her. He put a few extra shots of vodka in her drink when she wasn't looking. I wanted her to loosen up a bit. She was acting all stuck-up. Said she wasn't interested, but I know she was. They all are in Vegas. That's why they're here. To have a good time.'

Luiz bared his teeth like a wolf against a rival. 'You come anywhere near her again and I'll make sure you're sipping your meals through a straw for the rest of your life. Understood?'

The man nodded as he rubbed at his throat, slinking away like a cowed animal until he disappeared into one of the elevators.

Luiz muttered a curse and bent down to where the English girl had slumped to the floor. He touched the side of her creamy cheek with a light fingertip. She was a ghastly shade of white and her skin was clammy but her breathing was normal. 'Are you staying in house?' he asked.

She blinked owlishly at him. 'Have we met before?'

'Briefly.'

She cocked her head and narrowed her gaze as if trying to place him. 'You look kind of familiar…'

'Your room number?' he prompted.

Her smooth brow wrinkled for a moment as he helped her to her feet. Luiz tried not to notice the way the skin of her hand felt against his, soft as the petals of a magnolia.

'I think it has a seven in it.' She gave him a bright smile. 'That's my lucky number. I once won a day spa package in a raffle we had at school. It was so relaxing I didn't want to leave. It was the first time I had a Brazilian. Belinda talked me into it. It hurt like hell. Funny thing is I get them all the time now. I guess my pain threshold has risen or something. Normally I'm the biggest coward out. I cry when I take a plaster off. It's pathetic.' Her dazzling smile faded a little as she added, 'I blame it on losing my mother so young. She died in an accident when I was ten…'

'I'm sorry to hear that—'

'My father never remarried,' she went on as if he hadn't spoken. 'I thought he would replace her as soon as he could, but no. He never did. Not that he hasn't had lovers. He's had lots and lots of them. No one ever likes to think of their parents doing it, do they? It's gross. My dad is over sixty. I mean, what *is* he thinking? Isn't it time to put his tackle away and have a rest?'

'I guess boys will be boys, no matter what their age.'

She gave him another angled look. 'Am I keeping you from something? Someone?'

'No.'

'No hot date?'

'Sadly, no.'

She scrunched up her forehead again. 'Why not?'

'I asked a girl to dance with me but she turned me down.'

She made a sympathetic sound. 'Oh, poor you. Were you terribly crushed?'

'Irreparably.'

She put a hand on his arm, sending a shock of electricity straight to his groin. 'Never mind. I'm sure you'll find someone some day. I think there's a soulmate out there for each of us. We just have to be patient and wait until the planets align. Or at least that's what I keep telling myself.'

Luiz momentarily lost his train of thought as he looked at the soft and generous bow of her mouth. Her lips were still glossy from a recent coating of lipgloss, making them look even more luscious and tempting. He could smell the flowery scent she wore, a mixture of gardenia and honeysuckle that teased his nostrils and made him think of sultry summer nights. 'How much did you have to drink?' he asked.

'Hardly anything. I'm not a big drinker. I talk too much when I have wine. I guess that's why it's called truth serum, huh? *In vino veritas.* That's Latin, by the way. The truth is in the wine.' She gave him another megawatt smile. 'That's why I stuck to vodka. One shot with orange juice and I didn't even get to finish it because I was too busy dancing. Did you see me? It was awesome. I've never been able to do the Macarena before.'

Luiz felt like a parent handling a wayward teenager after a night out on the town. 'Do you have your room key with you?'

She fished around in her purse, her brow doing that little crinkly thing again, her teeth embedded in her lower lip. After a fruitless search she dropped her purse and reached inside the left hand cup of her bra and handed him a card key with another broad smile. 'I knew I put it somewhere safe.'

Luiz could feel the heat of her breast on the card. His fingers moved over its surface in a stroking manner as he locked gazes with her. 'This card isn't from this hotel. Do you know which one you're staying at?'

She wrinkled her nose like a child refusing to eat spinach. 'I don't want to go *there*. This is much nicer.'

'Do you know where you are? What floor you're on?'

She gave him a vampish look, batting her impossibly long eyelashes coquettishly. 'I'm on *your* floor.'

He ignored the wanton come-on in her gaze on principle. He could have any woman he wanted. He didn't have to resort to drunk or stoned ones. He might be considered an irascible rake but even *he* had some standards. 'Listen, *querida*, you need to lie flat in a dark room until you sober up.'

She pushed her lush mouth out in a pout. 'I'm not drunk. Look, I can walk in a straight line.' She tottered off along the corridor, arms out wide to stabilise her passage. She turned and came back towards him but the fourth step was her undoing. Her legs suddenly tangled and she came down in a heap and would have fallen badly if not for him catching her in time.

He gathered her slim body in his arms, trying not to notice the sweet cinnamon of her breath on his face as she snuggled up close with her arms flung around his neck. 'I'm soooo tired…' She gave a huge yawn and dropped her head against the wall of his chest and closed her eyes with a soft little sigh.

He gave her a gentle shake. 'Hey, you didn't tell me your name.'

She made another soft purring sound and burrowed closer to his chest. 'Need to sleep now…'

Luiz caught sight of himself carrying his rescued damsel in one of the gilt mirrors hanging above the hall table. Her shiny shoulder-length hair was swaying loose in a soft cloud over one of his arms, tickling the skin where he had rolled back the cuffs of his shirt. Her conservative black dress had ridden up, revealing slim legs and thoroughbred-narrow ankles, and a soft dreamy smile curved her mouth as her cheek settled against the steady beat of his heart as if she had finally found home.

He let out a low rough expletive. 'Now what, Sir Galahad?'

CHAPTER TWO

DAISY WOKE WITH a construction site hammering inside her head. Her mouth felt as if she had been sucking on a gym sock all night and her stomach was churning so fast it could have spat out pats of butter.

She cranked open one eye to find herself in a plush penthouse suite instead of her budget book-three-nights-get-one-free hotel room. Chandeliers dripped from the high ceiling in a waterfall of sparkling and twinkling crystal. The walls were papered in a luxurious satin-embossed two-toned stripe that was unapologetically masculine and yet opulently stylish. The lighting was softly muted but she could see a sliver of bright sunlight through the gap in the brocade curtains, suggesting it was well past dawn. The acre of carpet looked so thick she was sure if she took one step on it she would be knee-deep. Maybe neck-deep. The pillows behind her were as soft as clouds and the sheets that covered her naked body were super-fine Egyptian cotton.

Her stomach swooped. *Naked* body? She lifted the sheet and peeked beneath it. *Eek!* She'd had sex with someone? No. Not possible. Not in a million squillion years. She was not the type of girl to go to bed with a stranger. She hadn't even gone to bed with a friend. Flirting was one thing. Sharing her body with someone was something else again. But why on earth would she be naked in bed if she hadn't?

No. No. No.

Surely she hadn't. *Had* she? She pressed her legs together. *Nope. Doesn't feel any different.* She checked her breasts for any love bites. Scrambled up onto her knees to glance in the mirror to see if her neck had any signs of foreplay.

Nothing.

The door of the bedroom opened and Daisy choked out a shocked gasp and quickly cupped her hands over her breasts as Luiz Valquez with his laughing black eyes entered the room. '*You?*'

He gave a mock formal bow. 'At your service, *mi pasión.*'

His...passion? Double eek! Daisy dived under the sheets, pulling them right up to her chin. Oh, dear God. What had she done? Or, more to the point… What had *he* done? Anger came to her rescue, filling her voice with fulminating rage. 'Where are my clothes?'

The half-smile that tilted his mouth had a glint of devilry about it. 'Where you left them.'

Her eyes widened in horror. Had he—*gulp*—stripped her? Stolen her clothes? Was she to be sold into sex slavery? Never to be heard from again? Where was her damn bodyguard when she needed him? She threw Luiz a combative glare, determined not to show how terrified she was. 'I won't let you get away with this. You don't know who you're dealing with. I have connections that could wipe the floor with you.'

He had the gall to chuckle. 'You mean those two travelling companions of yours?'

Daisy felt her flesh shrink on her bones. Oh, dear Lord. What if Belinda and Kate had been kidnapped as well? Were all three of them to be shipped off to some ghastly foreign hellhole where disgusting men would paw and slaver over them? She could already see the headlines. *Three London Infant Teachers: Tragic Victims of International Sex Slave Ring.* 'Wh-what about them?'

His dark eyes gave nothing away other than amusement. 'They weren't the least bit interested in coming to your rescue.'

She narrowed her gaze to slits. 'What do you mean?'

'I asked them to fetch you from my suite last night but they refused.'

Daisy shot him a look of pure venom. 'I don't believe you. They would never leave me to fend for myself.' *Hmm, maybe Belinda would.* 'Anyway, how did you contact them? You didn't have their numbers or names.'

He inspected his square and buffed nails in a casual manner. 'I sent a staff member to find them. Apparently they were too busy with their dates to come and collect you.' He looked at her again and added, 'Their message to you was—and I quote—"Have fun".'

I am so going to kill you, Belinda.

Daisy huddled further up the bank of pillows under her shroud of luxury sheets. He looked so…so unlike a sexual predator. He was too sophisticated. Too clock-stopping handsome. Why would he have to resort to kidnap when he could crook his little finger and have any woman he wanted? *Except you*, she thought as she recalled her haughty rejection of him in the bar. She swallowed to clear the ropey knot of part dread, part excitement currently clogging her throat. She had spent the night with one of the world's most notorious bad boys. How had he changed her mind? And why couldn't she remember a single second of it? 'What happened last night?'

He hooked an ink-black eyebrow upwards. 'You don't remember?'

She frantically hunted through her memory but it was like rifling through a file that hadn't been organised properly. Nothing made sense. She could only remember watching him for most of the night, feeling annoyed he was never without a partner. He seemed to be flaunting them before her every time she looked at him, doing raunchy dance moves with an array of nubile young women.

It was nauseating.

Daisy had staunchly remained a wallflower—her default position—until a compatriot from Ealing had asked her to dance. She hadn't really wanted to dance with him but she must have changed her mind for she remembered being on the dance floor and at one point cannoning into Luiz. The shockwave of touching his hard male body had sent her senses spinning like a top. His dark eyes had run over her partner in a sizing up look and his top lip had curled as if to say, *Is that the best you could do?* But after that her memory was a blank.

She gave him a caustic glare. 'Why did you bring me here?'

He sent his gaze over her in a long lazy sweep. 'You can't guess?'

In spite of her trepidation, Daisy felt every pore of her skin flower open in response. Heat rushed along her veins, lighting a fire that fanned out from her core. Damn the man for being so attractive. How shameful of her to be so turned on by such a fiend. No wonder her father thought she needed a bodyguard. Clearly she was a ticking time bomb when left to her own devices. One night let loose on the town and she hooked up with the world's most wicked playboy. 'Did you—' she swallowed tightly again '—undress me?'

His expression was now deadpan. 'No.'

Daisy looked at him blankly. 'Then who did?'

'You did.'

Her eyes were so wide with shock they felt as if they were going to pop out of her head. She hadn't been naked in front of anyone since she was twelve. She was twenty-six years old and she still got dressed under a towel at the gym. Body issues had plagued her since she hit puberty. Small breasts, a jelly belly if she didn't do a hundred sit-ups a day and thighs that had a tendency to look like cottage cheese if she didn't stick to her diet of cottage cheese. 'I don't believe you.'

A glimmer of a smile came back in his eyes. 'I thought you said you were a teacher. Where did you learn the stripper routine?'

'You're lying!' she choked. 'I would never do something like that!'

'It was the best lap dance I've ever had and I didn't even have to tip for it.'

Daisy felt a blush move over her face like a flame let loose beneath her skin. 'I don't believe you. You're making this up.' You must be. You *have* to be.

He shrugged as if he didn't give a damn either way. 'You want some breakfast before you leave?'

Daisy frowned in a combination of confusion and an inexplicable sense of disappointment. *He was letting her go?* 'You mean you're not going to keep me here chained to the bed to have your wicked way with me?'

Those sinfully dark eyes roved over her huddled form once more, sending another wave of heat to her core. 'Thanks, but no.'

She knew it was inconsistent of her to feel slighted but surely she hadn't been that much of a flop in bed? Sure, she might have been unconscious, but still... 'Fine. I'm leaving.' She scrambled off the bed, taking the sheet with her. 'If you'll lead me to my clothes I'll be right on my way.'

'They're on the coffee table near the sofa. I took the liberty of having them cleaned while you were sleeping.'

Daisy swung around to face him, a dangerous manoeuvre given she was mummy-wrapped in one of his sheets. She would have gone over except one of his hands shot out to steady her. It was warm and strong against her flesh, his fingers like velvet-covered steel. Something flashed through her brain...a vague memory of strong arms holding her close. Protectively close.

Fresh-smelling laundry detergent and lemon-scented male flesh close to her face. A rock-steady heartbeat. A sense of being carried to safety… She frowned to bring the memory closer but it floated away like an apparition that no longer wanted to be seen.

She craned her head right back to look into his eyes, her stomach folding over at the satirical gleam that permanently shone there. 'Why did you do that?'

'Have your clothes cleaned?'

'Yes.'

'Seemed the right thing to do under the circumstances.'

'What…erm, circumstances?'

His mouth had that half smiling slant to it again. 'After the lap dance you had an episode of dispensing with the contents of your stomach in my bathroom. Unfortunately, your aim was off.'

Oh, dear Lord above. Could this nightmare get any worse? 'I was…sick?'

'Spectacularly so.'

Daisy chewed her lower lip, desperately trying not to picture how *that* might have played out. No one looked their best when being sick. But it was the ultimate humiliation to have disgraced herself in front of *him*. He was so self-assured. So suave. How he must have gloated over her misfortune after the way she had rejected his offer of a dance. He couldn't have asked for a better comeuppance for her. She had been so dismissive of his warning the night before. Arrogant even. How had she been so stupid and trusting to let something like that happen? *Ugh!* She was not some silly young girl on her first night on the town. She had a university degree, for God's sake.

She rummaged inside her purse for a handful of banknotes, thrusting them at him. 'I'm terribly sorry for any inconvenience I've caused. I hope this covers the expense of...erm, seeing to my needs.' *Bleah. Bad choice of words.*

He pushed her hand back with a gentle but firm pressure, his eyes locked on hers. 'I don't want your money.'

Daisy was having trouble concentrating. Her thoughts were flying all over the place. The energy coming from his hand where it was holding hers back was making her whole body fizz with reaction. It was like being plugged into a power outlet with too high a voltage for her sensitive wiring. She was going to short circuit for sure. He was so intensely male. So unbelievably handsome it made a hollow space inside her belly vibrate. Her eyes kept tracking to his mouth. Had he kissed her? How annoying she couldn't remember. That was a mouth that would know how to kiss. There would be no teeth scraping and nose bumping and awkward repositioning of lips and tongues. That was a mouth that knew how to seduce, to slay her senses with one brush of those hard male lips against hers. She drew in a shaky little breath and pushed back against his hand. 'Take it. I insist.'

He pushed back a little harder. The uptake of tension triggered something deep and low in her pelvis. She felt it between her thighs, a tight ache that was part pulse, part contraction. A frisson shimmied down her spine as his fingers wrapped around hers, tethering her to him.

His hands were not smooth but slightly calloused, which was strangely arousing. His thumb found her pulse and measured its frantic pace. 'I have plenty of money.'

Daisy gave him an imperious look to disguise the catastrophic effect he was having on her senses. 'Is that supposed to impress me?'

A lazy smile teased up the corners of his mouth. 'Nothing else has so far.'

She raised one of her eyebrows. 'You mean I wasn't left breathless and gasping by your…erm, attentions last night?'

He gave a deep chuckle, which combined with that toe-curling stroking along the thumpety-thump-thump-thump of her pulse, made her senses careen off into another tailspin. 'Your honour was safe with me, *dulzura*. I didn't lay a finger on you.'

Daisy pulled out of his hold, blinking at him in surprise. 'Y-You didn't?'

He shook his head with mock gravitas.

'Why not?'

'I prefer my women sober.'

She glared at him again, stamping her foot for good measure. 'I was not drunk! I've never been intoxicated in my life.'

'You were legless last night. Just as well I came along when I did. You were about to get down and dirty with the man in Suite 1524.'

Daisy stopped glaring at him. Another fragmented memory filtered through the haze of her brain. The guy from Ealing pressuring her to have a drink. Refusing his offer but finding he had bought her one while she had gone to the restroom. He insisting he keep her company while she drank it. She had suffered his company because she'd become so irritated with seeing Luiz Valquez working the room like Casanova with catnip. Surely a single vodka and orange wouldn't have caused her to lose all sense of control? 'How do you know I was going to…erm, become intimate with that guy? I might've just been going to his room to—'

'Look at his etchings?'

She gave him a look. 'Not all men have one-track minds, you know.'

He moved over every inch of her sheet-wrapped body with the smouldering heat of his gaze. 'They do when someone looks as gorgeous as you.'

Daisy knew it was a throwaway line but she couldn't help feeling a little thrill all the same. It wasn't that she wasn't used to compliments. She knew she wasn't model-thin or billboard-beautiful but she was pretty enough in a girl-next-door sort of way. But hearing him say it made her feel all fluttery and feminine. It made her want to flirt with him, which was rather surprising as she never flirted.

She shuffled over to where her clothes were folded in a neat pile on a coffee table next to one of the plush sofas. 'I have to get moving. The girls will be waiting for me.' She scooped up her clothes with her free hand, turning back to glance at him. 'Do you mind if I use your bathroom to get changed?'

His eyes had that laughing glint in them again. 'Be my guest.'

Daisy sniffed the air in the luxuriously appointed

bathroom for any trace of sickness. To her very great relief it smelt of citrus with a hint of lemongrass and ginger. She unwrapped herself from the sheet and quickly donned her clothes, her fingers tracing over the lace of her bra and knickers as she thought of Luiz handling her intimates, even to pass them over to the laundry staff. Had he put her to bed? Had he carried her or had she walked/stumbled/crawled on her own? Had he tucked her in? A shiver passed over her flesh at the thought of his hands on her naked body. Damn it. Why couldn't she remember the most exciting moment of her life? If *he* hadn't acted inappropriately given the way he said *she* had, then why not? Wasn't he supposed to be a bad boy or something?

Or did he have some scruples after all?

When Daisy came out of the bathroom he was standing with his back to her, looking down at the Vegas strip in all its crazy madness. 'Are you decent?' he asked.

'Hardy-ha-ha.'

He grinned as he turned around to face her. 'Don't you like your men with a sense of humour?'

Her men? What a laugh. If only he knew the only men in her life were her father, her bodyguard and Robert, the elderly gardener at Wyndham Heath.

Daisy was afraid she was starting to like Luiz Valquez a little too much. His uncharacteristic chivalry was potently attractive. If what he had said was true about her having been in danger of being taken advantage of by the Ealing guy, she owed him a huge debt of gratitude, not censure. Anything could have happened to her last night but he had stepped in and made sure she was safe, possibly putting himself at risk in the process. She'd had him pegged as a hard partying bad boy and yet he had acted with honour and propriety.

Had the world got it wrong about him? Or did he cash in on his racy reputation because it fitted the image of the sporting superstar? Who was he behind that mask of sophisticated playboy? If she had offered herself to him so shamelessly and he'd refused, then he must surely have far more to him than met the eye.

She held her purse in front of her stomach with both hands, suddenly feeling terribly gauche…well, even more so than usual. 'About last night…' she began.

'Don't mention it. I won't.' Another glinting look. 'It can be our little secret.'

She gnawed her lip as she thought of all the thousands of followers he would have on Twitter or other social media. He could make an absolute fool of her with a couple of hash tags. What if he'd taken pictures of her without her knowing? Her stomach dropped. The stripper routine. *Oh, God.* What if he'd recorded it? Uploaded it? Sent it out to cyberspace. What if he blackmailed her? What if—?

He reached into his trouser pocket and handed her his phone. 'You can check it if you like.'

Daisy stared at his phone as if it were a grenade with the pin pulled out. 'I really don't think that's—'

'Here, I'll show you.' He came and stood shoulder to shoulder with her, accessing the camera roll on his phone. 'See?'

She peered at the images he was scrolling through,

conscious of the way his light lemony and citrus cologne sharpened the air. She could feel the slightest brush of his hair-roughened arm against her smoother one. Her traitorous mind began assembling images of them in bed together, limbs entangled, lips locked, tongues mating. 'Good gracious, is that a dress that girl is almost wearing?'

He gave one of his deep rumbly chuckles that sent her senses spinning all over again. 'For a simple scrap of fabric it was damn hard to get off.'

Daisy gave him a wry glance. 'What? She didn't offer to help you?'

'Can't remember.' He carried on thumbing through another few photos.

'How long ago was it—erm, she?'

'Ages ago.' He flashed her a sudden grin. 'A couple of weeks at least.'

Daisy rolled her eyes and then pointed to a picture on the photo stream of a slightly older woman standing next to Luiz at what looked like a cocktail party. 'Who's that?'

'My mother, Eloise.'

Something about the way he said his mother's name alerted her to an undercurrent of tension. 'She looks very beautiful. Very glamorous. Like a movie star.'

His lips moved in the semblance of a smile. 'Yes, she likes the spotlight, that's for sure.'

'You're not close?'

He looked at her briefly, his eyes meshing with hers in a moment of silence. There was a vacancy in the back of his gaze, as if he was looking in the past for something but was having trouble finding it. 'We were once, or so I thought.'

'When was that?'

He clicked off the screen of his phone and slipped it back into his pocket in a *subject closed* manner. 'What do you normally eat for breakfast?'

'*Well*…ideally, I would eat an egg white omelette and drink a herbal tea.'

His brow lifted. 'Ideally?'

She gave him a self-deprecating look. 'I'm rubbish at sticking to diets. I last about three days and then I cave in and eat everything that isn't nailed down.'

'How does bacon and eggs, pancakes, maple syrup and a side of hash browns sound?'

Daisy swayed on her feet as if about to go into a swoon. 'Like heaven. I'm so hungry I could eat a horse and chase the rider.'

He stood looking down at her with a gleaming look in his dark as pitch eyes. 'I've heard there are some riders out there who like to do all the chasing.'

Daisy held his look with an aplomb she had no idea she possessed. Who knew flirting could be so much fun? 'Then perhaps those riders should make sure they never get caught.'

He picked up a lock of her hair and twirled it a couple of times around his tanned finger. She felt the gentle tug as one by one the roots of her hair lifted off her scalp. His eyes slipped to her mouth, lingered there as if he was weighing up whether to kiss her or not.

Do it. Do it. Do it, a voice chanted in her head.

His head came down in a slow motion action, blocking out the light shining in from the window. He stopped a mere millimetre away from her mouth, close enough for their breaths to mingle. His smelt of toothpaste. God alone knew what hers smelt like after a night on the tiles. Bathroom ones included. *Ack!*

Daisy put a fingertip against his lips, her voice coming out as little more than a husky whisper. 'Wait.'

He nibbled her fingertip with his lips, making her legs unlock at the knees. 'What for?'

'I haven't even told you my name.'

He turned her hand over and kissed a tickling pathway from her wrist to her elbow. 'So, tell me.'

She shivered as his lips came back down to the sensitive skin on the underside of her wrist. 'Daisy...Daisy Wyndham.'

He held her wrist to his mouth as his eyes meshed with hers. 'Nice.'

Daisy had trouble breathing. His eyes were so dark she felt as if she were drowning in their bottomless depths. His stubble-surrounded mouth against her skin was making her belly do somersaults worthy of a Cirque du Soleil performance. She even heard the rasp of his skin as he moved his mouth to the heel of her hand as his tongue made one flicking lick against the ridge of flesh. A flashpoint of heat triggered a tumult of sensation in her core. She hadn't even realised that part of her hand had an erogenous zone.

The doorbell sounded behind him and he dropped her hand with a regretful smile. 'Breakfast.'

CHAPTER THREE

FOOD HAD NEVER been further from Daisy's mind, which was saying something as normally it was *always* on her mind. Forbidden food. The yummy stuff she secretly craved but rigorously denied herself in fear of losing control. Her father had drummed it into her from early childhood that being in control of one's mind and body and physical appetites was the mark of a well-disciplined person. In order to win his approval she denied herself anything that was the slightest bit sinful. But the years of self-denial hadn't made her stronger and more disciplined. If anything, they had made her all the more conflicted and confused about what she wanted and why she wanted it.

She watched with her mouth watering and her stomach rumbling as Luiz opened the door to the hotel attendant, who wheeled in a loaded trolley of silver domed dishes. The delicious aroma almost knocked her off her feet. Crispy bacon, soufflé-soft scrambled eggs, deep-fried hash browns, fluffy buttermilk pancakes, the sweetness of maple syrup—not the cheap imitation but the real stuff—a platter of tropical fruit, coffee and even a bottle of champagne in an ice bucket.

The attendant left with a sizeable tip in his hand, closing the door on his exit.

'*Wow.*'

Luiz tossed his wallet on the sofa. 'Hungry?'

'I meant the tip.' Daisy's eyes were still out on stalks. 'Did you really give that young man two hundred dollars?'

He shrugged a loose shoulder. 'I can afford it.'

'Do you light your cigarettes with a fifty?'

He flashed her a quick smile. 'I don't smoke.'

Another point in his favour, she thought as he began to take the lids off the food. He handed her a plate. 'Help yourself.'

Daisy tried to be circumspect. She *really* tried. But the food was so scrumptious and she hadn't had a proper cooked breakfast in years. Before she knew it, her plate was loaded with a mountain of monstrously wicked calories that would at some time in the future have to be worked off. But it would be worth it.

She took the chair opposite his at the table near the window overlooking the Nevada desert in the distance. She unwrapped her silver cutlery from the snowy white napkin it was encased in and then glanced across at Luiz but all he had in front of him was a steaming cup of black coffee. 'Aren't you hungry?'

'I'll have something later.'

'But there's so much here.' *Most of it on my plate.*

'I like to work out first.'

The gym or the bedroom? Daisy blushed as the

thought slipped into her mind. 'I suppose you have to be super fit to be a polo player.'

'If you want to be the best then that's exactly what you have to be.'

She looked up from her forkful of eggs. 'I've never been to a polo game. Is it fun?'

A smile kicked up the corner of his mouth. 'I enjoy it.'

'So…that's all you do? Fly around the world to play polo?'

'I have business interests with my older brother Alejandro. Resorts, investments, horse breeding, that sort of thing. But yes, I mostly fly around the globe to play polo.'

Daisy took a mouthful of the delectable bacon, trying not to groan in ecstasy as it went down. 'Don't you ever get bored?' she asked after a moment.

He cradled his coffee cup in one hand, the handle pointing away from him. 'How do you mean?'

'Living out of hotel rooms all the time. Doesn't that get a little boring year after year after year?'

Something about his expression subtly changed. The half smile was not so playful. The chiselled contours of his jaw not so relaxed. His eyes a little more screened than before. 'Not so far.'

'Don't get me wrong—' she scooped up some more egg '—I love hotel rooms, especially ones as nice as this. But there's no place like home.'

'Where do you live?'

'London.'

'Want to narrow that down a bit?'

Daisy gave him a coy look over her loaded fork. 'Why do you ask? Are you thinking of visiting me?'

His eyes didn't waver as they held hers. 'I don't do relationships, especially long distance ones.'

She squashed a little niggle of disappointment. Last night she had thought him the most obnoxious upstart. But now…

She gave a mental shrug and loaded up her fork again. 'I live in Belgravia.'

His brow lifted ever so slightly. 'So you're no stranger to money in spite of your comment about the tip earlier.'

Daisy gave him a sheepish glance. 'It's not my flat. It belongs to my father. I pay him a nominal rent. He insists I live in a high security complex. He's kind of overprotective, to put it mildly.'

He leaned forward to refill his cup from the silver percolator on the table. 'You're lucky to have someone watching out for you.'

Daisy wondered if he'd think she was so lucky if she told him the rest. Like how her father often turned up unannounced at her flat, checking her fridge or pantry for contraband food. Not to mention dates. Making comments about her clothes and appearance or the amount of make-up she was wearing. Offering his opinion on every aspect of her life. She had put up with his controlling ways for too long. The trouble was she had no idea how to get him to change without hurting him. So many of her friends didn't have fathers, or had fathers who weren't interested or involved in their lives. She had already lost one parent. The thought of losing another—even through estrangement—was too daunting.

She studied Luiz's face for a moment. 'You mentioned your mother. What about your father? Is he still alive?'

His expression gave the tiniest flinch as if the mention of his father was somehow painful to him. 'He died a couple of years ago.'

'I'm sorry.'

'Don't be.' He stirred his coffee with a teaspoon even though she hadn't seen him put sugar or cream into it. 'He was glad to go in the end.'

'Was he ill?'

'He had a riding accident when I was a kid. He wasn't expected to survive but he did—much to my mother's despair.'

Daisy frowned. 'But surely—?'

His expression was cynical. 'It wasn't my mother's idea of marital bliss to be shackled to a quadriplegic who couldn't even lift a cup to his mouth. She left six months after the accident.' He swirled the coffee in his cup until it became a dark whirlpool. Daisy watched with bated breath for some to spill over the sides but it didn't. It told her a lot about him. He was a risk-taker but he knew exactly how far he could push the boundaries.

'Did she take you and your brother with her?'

He laughed a brittle-sounding laugh. 'She hadn't wanted kids in the first place. She only married my father because her family pressured her into it once she got pregnant with my brother.' He put the cup down again with a precise movement before he sat back, hooking one ankle over the top of his muscled thigh. 'She came back a couple of years later to get me but our father wouldn't hear of it.'

'Would you have wanted to go?'

His lips rose and fell in a shrug-like movement. 'It was no picnic being brought up in a sickroom. My brother did his best but he wasn't able to be both parents and a brother to me. But I wouldn't go unless he came too and there was no way he would ever leave my father.'

'So you stayed.'

'I stayed.'

A silence crept in from the four corners of the room.

There was no outward sign on his face but Daisy got the impression he regretted revealing so much about his background. His fingers began to drum on the arms of the chair he was sitting on. It was barely audible but it spoke volumes. He wasn't a man to sit around chatting. He was a man of action. He lived life on the edge. He didn't sit on the sidelines and ruminate about what might have, could have, or should have been.

'Why did you come to my rescue last night?'

His eyes took on that teasing glint again but she noticed his smile looked a little forced. 'You seemed like a nice kid. I didn't want you to come to any harm on your first night in Vegas.'

'So you tucked me safely up in bed and gallantly slept on the sofa.'

'Correction. I didn't sleep.'

She frowned. 'What did you do?'

'I kept an eye on you.'

'Why?'

'Your drink was doctored. I heard it from the horse's mouth.'

Daisy's mouth dropped open. 'You mean a drug of some sort?'

'He only confessed to getting a friend to put a couple of extra shots of vodka in your glass while you weren't watching,' he said. 'I asked the hotel doctor to give you the once-over. He seemed pretty confident it was just a case of a little too much to drink. Your pupils and your breathing were normal.'

She stared at him with burgeoning respect. How had she got it so wrong about him? He had acted so responsibly last night. Taking care of her. Protecting her. Sacrificing his evening to stay with her. How had she thought he was shallow and arrogant? He wasn't the devil she had taken him for. He was a guardian angel. *Her* guardian angel. 'I don't know how to thank you for watching out for me.'

'Yeah, well, how about being a little more careful when you're out on the town? They're a lot of opportunistic guys out there who'd not think twice about taking advantage of a girl who's three sheets to the wind.'

Daisy chewed her lower lip. 'I can see now why my father always insists I travel with a bodyguard.'

His brows snapped together. 'You have a bodyguard?'

She gave him another sheepish look. 'I did up until last night. I slipped away from him to join the girls in the nightclub downstairs.'

'Where is he now?'

'Probably handing in his notice to my father.'

His frown cut into his forehead like a deep V. 'Don't you think you should call him to let him know you're safe?'

'I guess…'

He snatched up her purse where her phone was stored. 'Better do it before the cops put out a missing person's alert—if they haven't already.'

Daisy took out her phone to find thirty-three missed calls from her father. She had forgotten she'd put her phone on silent before she met the girls last night and hadn't got around to turning it back. She pressed the call button and mentally counted to three to prepare herself for the fallout. 'Dad?'

'Where the hell are you?' her father blasted. 'I've been worried sick. I was about to get every cop in Vegas out looking for you. Are you all right? What happened last night? Bruno told me you gave him the slip. Just wait until I see you, young lady. Do you think I'm not serious about your safety? There are creeps out there just waiting to get their hands on a good old-fashioned girl like you. I swear to God if anyone's hurt my baby girl I'll have their balls for breakfast.'

'I'm fine, Dad, please stop shouting.' Daisy tried to cover the mouthpiece but it was obvious Luiz had heard every word because he was grinning. 'I'm fine, really I am. Nothing happened. Nothing at all.'

'Where are you?' her father demanded.

'I'm at a hotel with a…a friend.'

'Which friend? You don't know anyone in Vegas apart from those silly girlfriends of yours.'

'A new friend.' Daisy looked at Luiz with a can-I-mention-your-name? look but, before he could give her an answer, she told her father, 'I'm with Luiz Valquez, you know, the famous polo champion?'

'*What?*' her father roared.

'I met him last night. He was terribly nice and took me to his—'

'That profligate time-wasting party boy?' Her father was apoplectic. 'Wait till I get my hands on him. I'll tear him limb from—'

Luiz signalled for her to give him the phone. 'I'll talk to him.'

Daisy gingerly handed the phone to him as her father continued his audible tirade. 'Sorry,' she mouthed.

'Mr…er…Wyndham? Luiz Valquez. Daisy was a little under the weather last night so I—'

'Drunk?' her father exploded. 'How dare you suggest such a thing? Do you have any idea of whom you're dealing with here?'

Luiz's mouth developed a smirk, which Daisy was eminently glad her father couldn't see. 'Yes, sir, I do. You're a loving father who is concerned about his daughter's welfare.'

She grimaced. Her father *hated* being patronised. She waited for the fallout. Any second now… She exchanged a quick look with Luiz. He wasn't looking unduly worried. If anything, there was a glint of amusement in his dark gaze.

'*Parli italiano?*' her father demanded.

'*Sì.*'

The rest of the exchange was conducted in rapid-fire Italian and, while Daisy was moderately good at languages, she wasn't *that* good. Whatever was said was short and to the point. Luiz showed little emotion on his face but she noticed the smirk had gone by the time the call ended and he handed back her phone. 'Quite a guy.'

'He's really sweet when you get to know him.'

There was a pregnant silence.

'What did he say to you?' Daisy asked.

'Nothing much.'

She chewed her lip again. Her father could be quite threatening at times. He was all bluster, of course. He wouldn't hurt a fly if push came to shove. She reached for her purse again. 'I guess I should let you get on with your morning.'

Luiz's hand on her arm stalled her. 'There'll be press out there.'

'Press?'

His look was grim. 'Paparazzi. They follow me everywhere.'

'Oh…' Daisy hadn't got as far as thinking beyond leaving his hotel suite before she made a complete fool of herself and begged him to kiss her. Being in his company had been far more pleasant than she'd expected. He was funny and charming and his gallantry towards her had totally ambushed her determination to dislike him. 'What should I do?'

'Leave all the talking to me.'

Daisy had spent most of her life having her voice silenced by her father. She wasn't going to let another man, even one as gorgeous and sexy as Luiz Valquez, speak for her. For the moment she'd play along but he would soon find out she wasn't as wet behind the ears as he thought. 'What will you say to them?'

'I'll think of something.'

Something that might not reflect too well on her, Daisy thought. His scandalously racy reputation was well known. Being found in his room was not going to do hers any favours. She would be painted as one of his groupies for sure. No way was she going to be portrayed as yet another one of his one-night stands. She would have to think of something a little more fitting for a London kindergarten teacher who had the school board to consider.

Luiz reached for the champagne in the ice bucket. 'Have a drink with me.'

'At this hour?'

He popped the cork and poured the delicate bubbles into the crystal long-stemmed flutes. He handed her one, clinking his against hers in a toast. 'What happens in Vegas stays in Vegas.'

Daisy took a sip of the champagne, feeling decidedly decadent on top of her calorie-rich breakfast. 'Hair of the dog, huh?'

'Works for me.'

She watched as he took a measured sip of his drink. His smile had faded and two pleats had formed between his brows. 'Is something wrong?'

His features relaxed but she could still see a faint line of tension around his mouth. 'What are your plans for the rest of your stay? Have you booked any tours?'

'No, the girls have but I wanted to do my own thing.

I hate structured tours. I like to mooch around and get a feel for the place on my own.'

'Fancy me as a guide for the next couple of hours?'

Daisy fancied him full stop. Big time. The longer she spent in his company, the more tempted she was to relax her good girl standards and take a walk on the wild side with him. Besides, hadn't he already demonstrated his trustworthiness? What would be the harm in hanging out with him for the rest of the day? Maybe even a few days?

A little thought took hold in her mind… She could have a holiday fling with him to get herself out there. He wasn't interested in anything permanent. And there was no way she could ever be serious about someone so unsuitable as husband material. But for a few days of flirting and fun…who better than a man who really knew how to lay on the charm? 'Are you sure you're not too busy?'

'For you, *querida?*' He clinked his glass against hers once more, his black eyes gleaming. 'I am more than happy to clear my diary.'

'Well…if you insist.'

'I do.'

She smiled at him. 'You know something? When I first met you I thought you were brash and arrogant and ridiculously shallow.'

'And now?'

'I think underneath that easy come, easy go exterior you're a really nice guy.'

A dangerous light came back on in his eyes as he trailed a lazy finger down the curve of her cheek. 'Don't be fooled, little English girl. Your white knight has the blackest of hearts.'

'At least you have one.'

He studied her mouth for a heart-stopping moment. Daisy felt her breath come to a screeching halt as his fingertip traced the outline of her lips, the top one and then the bottom one. The movement of his finger stirred every nerve into a happy dance. She could feel her lips buzzing as if a swarm of bees was trapped beneath their surface.

'Are you going to kiss me?' Had she *really* asked that? She really needed to work on her flirting lines. But hey, this might just be the opportunity to do it.

His mouth curved upwards in an enigmatic smile. 'Let's say I'm measuring the risks.'

'Just so you know...I don't bite.'

'No.' He took a fistful of her hair in his hand and pulled her close as his mouth came down towards hers. 'But I do.'

CHAPTER FOUR

HER LIPS WERE soft and pliable and she tasted of a heady cocktail of champagne and innocence. Luiz had wanted to kiss her from the moment he'd laid eyes on her in the nightclub. Her feisty little brush-off had amused him. He knew he could take her down given enough time. Now he had her in his arms but taking it a step further was giving him some pause. Her father had issued a thinly disguised warning. Sully his little girl's reputation and there would be unpleasant consequences. Luiz would have told him where to stick his threats but the name Charles Wyndham rang a faint alarm bell in his head.

But that didn't mean he couldn't indulge in a kiss with Daddy's little princess first.

Except that kissing her was proving to be far more addictive than he had bargained for. Her soft lips opened on a breathless sigh as he deepened the kiss with a smooth stroke of his tongue against the seam of her mouth. She pressed herself closer to his body, triggering a molten fire inside him as he recalled every deliciously naked inch of her last night as she had wantonly stripped off her clothes and danced and jiggled her breasts around him. In spite of his moral stance, it had taken a monumental amount of willpower to resist her clumsy attempt to seduce him. She had gorgeous curves that were womanly and yet delightfully youthful. Her breasts were small but perfect globes of feminine flesh with rose-pink nipples that had made his mouth ache to taste their budded peaks. Her waist was tiny in comparison to the feminine swell of her hips, small enough for his hands to span, which had been one temptation he hadn't been able to resist. He had done it as an experiment…or so he told himself. But feeling her push against him in nothing but her creamy skin had all but disabled his willpower. A backdraught of heat had shot through his system when her pelvis came in contact with his.

Luiz felt it again as she moved against him now and, even though this time she was fully clothed, just knowing that under that little black dress and those little lacy black knickers she was waxed clear made him throb with a fireball of lust.

He plunged deeper into her mouth, seeking the hot sweet wetness of her, as if that in some vicarious way would suffice. Her tongue approached his with a teasing little flicker that made him go after it with ruthless intent. He drew it into his mouth, cajoling it into submission as his hands gripped her hips and held her tight against the swell of his pounding erection. Need roared inside him like a wild animal on the prowl. Earthy need. Primal need that would not be assuaged any other way than with monkey sex at its most animated.

He brought his hands to her head, spreading his fingers through her hair as he held her mouth to his in a passionate duel. Not that she was fighting him or anything. She was with him all the way, making it impossible for him to pull back and get perspective.

Damn perspective.

He wanted her.

But, for all that, her father's threat sent a cube of ice scudding down his spine. It was one thing to make a threat to have his legs broken—which he didn't for a moment take seriously because last time he looked he wasn't in an episode of a mob drama—but how far did her old man's influence reach? During the course of the brief conversation Charles Wyndham had chillingly mentioned Alejandro and Teddy's upcoming wedding. They had married a few weeks earlier in a marriage of convenience arrangement to secure Teddy's inheritance and some land next to the Valquez family estate—now Alejandro's property—which had been swindled off their father by Teddy's father twenty years ago.

How much did Charles Wyndham know about the way Alejandro and Teddy had come together? Luiz knew Alejandro was at great pains to give Teddy the best wedding day imaginable, given he had marched her off to a register office for a civil ceremony that had no hint of romance or fairy tale about it. Charles Wyndham had implied Alejandro and Teddy's special day would be sabotaged if Luiz didn't play by the rules.

Rules. Schmules. No one told him what to do or how to do it.

But this wasn't just about him now. His older brother

had sacrificed years of his life—the best years—to salvage the family business and to bring Luiz up. Alejandro had forfeited fun for duty. Now he was finally happy with the lovely Teddy and all that could be undone if Luiz didn't watch his step.

As much as it galled him to appear to be kowtowing to a tyrannical dictator, he knew it was in his interests to keep things cool until this particular storm cloud blew over. All he had to do was hang out with Daisy for a few hours before getting her back on her way with her girlfriends.

After he finished kissing her, of course.

When had a kiss tasted so tantalising? Her arms were around his neck, her mouth pressed hotly to his, her fingers playing with the ends of his hair that brushed his collar. Shivers coursed up and down his spine at her touch. He imagined those soft little hands exploring other parts of his body: down the muscles of his back and shoulders, his chest and abdomen and lower, where he throbbed and pulsed the hardest.

He groaned deep in the back of his throat as her teeth nipped at his lower lip before salving the sting with a moist stroke of her cat-like tongue. His erection painfully hardened at the thought of that clever little tongue teasing the length of him, tasting him, taking him to the limit of human control and beyond.

Her body rubbed against him invitingly, from chest to thigh, ramping up his desire to a level that was quickly slipping out of the bounds of his normally cool and measured control. He prided himself—some would say arrogantly so—on being a supremely competent lover who always made sure a good time was had by all. But with Daisy's soft little mouth and her perky little breasts and her curvy body wreaking such havoc on his senses he felt like a trigger-happy teenager.

He pulled back reluctantly, his body instantly wailing at the loss of the teasing friction of hers. 'This might be a good time to put the brakes on.'

Her cheeks were flushed a deep shade of rose. Her lips were swollen from the press of his; even her chin had a little red patch where his morning stubble had caught her. She had a dazed look in her beautiful blue eyes. He suspected it might match the one he was doing his level best to disguise in his own. 'Oh…yes, right. Good idea…'

'Do you normally kiss like that?' he found himself asking.

Her forehead puckered. 'Was I totally rubbish at it?'

'Hell, no. I'm just saying…' What *was* he saying? That she knocked him off his feet with a kiss? Yeah, right, like he was going to tell her that. *Anyone* that.

She, it seemed, had no such scruples. 'You're an amazing kisser. No wonder you've got the reputation you have.'

Why did his reputation feel like something to be ashamed of when he was with her? He couldn't imagine her leaping from one bed to the other, barely taking enough time to register a sexual partner's name before moving on to the next.

Not that he wasn't happy with his life. His life was fun. He liked being on the move. Putting down roots was for trees. Not for him.

But something about the way she was looking at him made a space creak open inside his chest. A tiny fissure along a fault line, barely enough to send a beam of light through, but he felt a spill of warmth flow from it and brush like a puff of a hot breath against his chilled heart.

'What was wrong with the way I was kissing you?' she suddenly asked.

'Nothing. It was great. You were great. Fabulous, in fact.' He stopped gushing long enough to draw a breath to rebalance. 'You might want to hold back on the enthusiasm a bit. A less principled guy might take advantage of it.' *Jeez, he was starting to sound like a parent again.*

'But what if I wanted you to take advantage of it?'

Luiz blinked. 'No, you don't… *Do* you?'

Her face was so youthfully open and fresh it made something deep inside his chest pinch. 'I didn't before but I've changed my mind. I like you. I'd like to spend some more time with—'

'No. No. No. A thousand times no.' He practically frogmarched her to the door. 'You, young lady, need to go and join your friends. Go do a tour of the Grand Canyon or go shopping or book to see a show or something.' He scooped up her purse and thrust it in her hands before opening the door. 'Out.'

A blinding flash hit him in the eyes as a round of paparazzi cameras went off.

'Luiz, tell us about your mystery date,' a journalist said. 'Everyone's talking about her. Who is she?'

'Are you going to see her again?'

'What's your name, sweetheart?'

Luiz took Daisy's arm and pulled her back behind him. 'Don't tell them.'

'Ooh!' a female journalist crowed. 'It must be serious. He's never done *that* before.'

'Her name's Daisy,' someone offered from the back of the assembled press. 'I spoke to one of her friends earlier. She's a kindergarten teacher from a posh school in London.'

'Can we expect a double wedding with your brother, eh, Luiz?' one of the old regulars asked.

Luiz laughed it off. 'We're just friends.'

'How about we hear what Miss Wyndham has to say?'

Luiz's fingers clamped down on Daisy's wrist. 'She has no comment to make. Now, if you'll excuse us—'

'Yes, I do.' Daisy poked her head around his shoulder before he could stop her. 'I'm in love with Luiz and he's in love with me.'

Somehow Luiz kept his composure but it was a near thing. Thank God for the improvisation drama classes way back in his boarding school days. He smiled stiffly and put his arm around Daisy's waist, tugging her close to his body; registering again how neatly she fitted against him. 'That's right.' He swallowed to get his next words out without choking. 'We're officially a couple.'

The cameras went crazy. So many flashes and clicks it sounded like rounds of artillery on a battlefield.

But this was one battle Luiz was determined to win. No one—not even a pretty little English girl or her overbearing father—was going to manipulate him into a relationship. He was a free agent and he was going to stay that way.

He shepherded Daisy back inside his suite and closed the door firmly, hoping the paparazzi would get the message and move on. When he was certain they had left he nailed her with a hardened look. 'Want to tell me what that was all about?'

She stood before him, straight-backed and defiant. 'I didn't want them to think I was one of your groupies.'

'*In love?*' Saying the words felt as if he was coughing up a fur ball.

Her cheeks stained with spreading colour. 'OK, I admit it might've been a bit over the top but I had to say something.'

'No, you did not.' He didn't bother softening his tone. 'I told you to keep quiet. But no. You go and announce to the world you're in love with me. *Seriously?*'

A combative light came into her eyes. 'It's all right for you. You don't care what people think of you, but I have to think of my reputation. I don't want to be seen as another one of your trashy one-night stands. I have children who look up to me.'

He looked at her blankly. 'Children?'

She whooshed out a flustered breath. 'My pupils. You heard what the journalist said. My school's not just your common or garden variety one. The parents pay extortionate fees to have their little darlings educated. As a staff member I have standards to uphold both professionally and personally. Kindergarten kids are highly impressionable. If word got back to the school board that I was cavorting in Vegas with a layabout play—'

'Hey, watch your language.'

She rolled her eyes. 'Whatever.'

Luiz raked a hand through his hair. Did she really think he was—? No, don't even go there. He didn't care what she thought of him. Why would he? He didn't have to explain himself to her or to anyone. 'I don't care if you want to pretend to be in love with me, but why throw in that porkie of me being in love with you?'

She gave him a pert look. 'How do you know I'm pretending?'

He narrowed his gaze. 'You're…you're not serious?'

She flashed him a teasing smile. 'No, of course not. You're the last person I'd ever fall for.'

'Why?' *You so should not have asked that.*

She put a finger to her lips, tapping them thoughtfully. 'Let me count the ways…' She held up each finger as she ticked them off. 'You're arrogant. Overly confident. Egotistical. Self-serving. Morally corrupt.'

Luiz let out a hissing breath, following it up with a choice expletive. 'I should've left you to that sleazeball last night. That's who I'd be calling morally corrupt.' Along with her mob-connected father, a fact he declined to mention because, as angry as he was, he wasn't the type of guy to judge her for who her parents were or what they did.

'Why are you so upset?' she asked. 'It's not as if I'm rushing you to the nearest wedding chapel for an Elvis-themed wedding or something.'

He swung round to fix her with another glare. 'I'm the one with the reputation being trashed here. You're making me out to be some sort of soppy, heartsore

Romeo who's gone gaga over a girl he didn't know from a bar of soap this time yesterday.'

'What did I tell you?' She flickered her eyelids upwards again. 'Self-serving and egotistical.'

He jabbed a finger towards her. 'Hey, wait a damn minute. I've a right to be a little pissed. I did the right thing by you and now it's coming back to bite me.'

Her pert look was back. 'Maybe you should've taken advantage of me when you had the chance.'

A vision of her gloriously naked and trying to climb into his skin flooded his brain. His groin remembered it all too well. It was responding in the only way it knew how. Instinctively. Urgently. He sent her a smouldering look and watched as her cheeks darkened. 'Don't tempt me, *mi pasión.*'

The tip of her tongue crept out to leave a shiny film of moisture over her youthful mouth. His mouth recalled every passionate movement of hers underneath his: the soft fullness, the sweetness, and the ripeness. 'It'd be fine if you want to,' she said. 'Sleep with me, I mean.'

He frowned at her. 'I thought you said I was a self-serving, egotistical jerk?'

'You are, but that doesn't mean I don't fancy you.'

Luiz shook his head, hoping it would get his addled brain in order. 'Let me get this straight… You *want* me to have a one-night stand with you?'

She put her hands on her hips as if she were addressing one of her infant charges. 'You're not listening to me, Luiz. I'm not interested in a one-night stand. I'm not that sort of girl. I will, however, agree to a short-term holiday fling.'

His frown was so deep it was making his forehead hurt. 'So what was with the sweet little romance thing just now? Why give the press the impression we're in—' he refused to say the word *love* again in case it jinxed him '—an item? Why not say we're having a fling?'

'It's not just the school board I have to consider. I have my father to think about. If the press wrote that I stumbled out of your suite and never saw you again he'd be after your blood. Not literally, of course. But he'd be furious if I were to waste myself on someone who didn't appreciate me. He's old-fashioned like that.'

'You don't say.' He sent his hand through his hair again. If this farce got any crazier he'd be pulling it out by the clump.

'I'm only here for four days,' she said. 'That's long enough to have a holiday romance and then move on. Dad will understand these flash in the pan things don't always last. And hopefully now we've made our announcement to the press they'll leave us alone.'

He studied her for a long moment. 'So, let me get this straight. You want to have a fling with me. For four days and nights. No strings?'

She smiled brightly as if he had just explained relativity to her after a painfully slow lesson. 'Exactly.'

'But why?'

'Why what?'

'Why me?'

'I told you before. I like you.'

'Even though I'm a morally corrupt layabout?'

She gave a tinkling bell laugh that did serious damage to his resolve to send her on her way as soon as he could. It was a champagne laugh. A bubbly, happy sound that made him think of fun and celebration. Her smile was the same—bright and positive, a smile that in full force made the hot Nevada desert sun look dull.

'I guess lust doesn't discriminate, does it?' she said.

It certainly does not, Luiz thought. If he'd known she was going to be this much trouble he would never have asked her to dance, much less come to her rescue.

Maybe that wasn't strictly true…

He could have no more left her in that corridor than fly to the moon on a paper aeroplane. Daisy was the sort of girl he instinctively wanted to protect. His brother had done a good job on him. Alejandro was the master at the white knight gig; the way he cosseted his wife Teddy was proof of it. Luiz was happy for his brother finding love. He hadn't thought it would ever happen. But that didn't mean *he* was looking for a similar happy ending. He didn't do happy endings. He couldn't rely on them. He was all about living in the moment.

And right now he had a hell of a moment to get through.

Luiz strode over to the window to check if any more press had turned up outside the hotel complex. He could feel Daisy's clear blue gaze studying him from behind. Never had a woman's presence disturbed him so much. She was sweet and innocent and yet impossibly sexy, a potent combination he had never encountered before. The taste of her kiss lingered in his mouth like a delectable dessert he hadn't had enough of. His taste buds were zinging, his lips buzzing, his blood thrumming. Last night had been the first time he had spent the night with a woman without making love to her. The need to do so was still thundering in his body. But it wasn't just the lust that worried him. The spill-all conversation over breakfast… *Why had he done that?* What was it about her that made him reveal so much about his past?

'So, what's the plan?' she said in an eager voice. 'What are we doing today?'

He twitched the curtains back across the window and faced her. 'How many lovers have you had?'

She momentarily sank her teeth into the pillow of her lower lip. 'Depends what you mean by lover.'

His brows met over his eyes. 'Have you had sex?'

'Technically, yes, but not with a human.'

No wonder her old man didn't let her out without a SWAT-trained security team, Luiz thought. 'Want to elaborate?'

Her cheeks were a fiery red but her blue eyes were unapologetic as they held his. 'A girl has the right to pleasure herself if there's no one else about. You men do it all the time. It's perfectly normal. A vibrator is good practice for the real thing…or that's what I'm hoping.'

Luiz was having trouble keeping his jaw off the floor. 'Are you saying you've never had sex other than with a vibrator?'

She gave him a huffy look. 'What of it? It's safe. At least I won't pick up any nasty infections. And he doesn't cheat on me.'

'He?'

'Edward.'

'You called your vibrator *Edward?*'

'What's wrong?' she said. 'It's a good old-fashioned

name. I admit it's a bit on the conservative side but I didn't want to sleep with a nameless object. It's… dehumanising.'

Luiz couldn't hold back a laugh. 'You are such a crazy girl. I don't think I've ever met anyone quite like you.'

'Same goes.'

'Meaning?'

She gave him a forthright look. 'You're so confident and upfront about what you want. Some would say brazen.'

'I thought you didn't like that about me?'

'Not if you were to be my life partner, but as a casual fling candidate you're perfect because it would be well-nigh impossible to damage your hubris.'

Luiz wasn't sure if she was insulting him or complimenting him. He wasn't sure why he even cared either way. 'So you ultimately want a life partner?'

Her expression was completely guileless. 'Doesn't everyone?'

'Not me.'

'Why not you?'

He lifted a shoulder. 'You said it yourself. I'd make a terrible husband.'

'You could be trained.'

He gave a wry laugh. 'You make me sound like a wild animal.'

Her beautiful blue eyes twinkled. 'Don't worry. I won't be in your life long enough to domesticate you.'

Something about the way she was calling the shots sat uncomfortably with him. He was the one who did the checking in and checking out. He didn't leave it to other people to come and go in his life. That was his prerogative. 'Why me?' he asked. 'Why not the other guy?'

'The Ealing guy?'

'Yeah. Him.' Luiz could barely think of that creep without wanting to punch something. Preferably him. Hard.

'I can't have a holiday fling with a compatriot. It's not half as exciting or exotic.'

'I'm not sure I've been called exotic before,' he muttered drily. 'Exciting, yes.'

She grinned at him. 'You're exotic to me because I've never even talked to an Argentinian before.'

'I can assure you we're situated on much the same level on the evolutionary chain as you Brits.'

'Oh, I wasn't implying you're not civilised,' she said sweetly. 'Look at how you conducted yourself last night. You were the perfect gentleman.'

'You only have my word on that.'

'Exactly my point.'

'I could be lying to you,' he said.

'But you're not.'

'You can tell that, how?'

'Your eyes,' she said, looking straight into them. 'You have the darkest brown eyes I've ever seen. But they don't shift about as if you're trying to hide something. And they laugh a lot. I find that really attractive. You look like a man who really enjoys life.'

Yeah, well, I was enjoying it just fine until a few hours ago, Luiz thought.

But had he?

Hadn't he come back to his suite alone because he *wasn't* enjoying himself?

He shrugged the thought aside. He had to find a way to get himself out of this entanglement before some serious harm was done.

Hadn't cute little Daisy Wyndham already got more out of him in a few minutes than anyone had in years? He *never* spoke of his childhood. To anyone. But for some reason he had spilled out his whole back story to her over breakfast. It had come pouring out...sentence after sentence, buried hurt after buried hurt. Little Miss Daisy Wyndham, with her sweet and engaging manner, had stumbled upon his Achilles heel. The pain and bitterness he concealed behind a laugh-at-life façade. He laughed his way through life because it was a damn sight more comfortable than whinging about the stuff he couldn't change.

He had been young—only eight years old—when his father had the accident, but not too young to understand that life would never be the same. He had spent day after day waiting for his mother to return from her 'holiday', as she'd termed it. He had almost worn out the end of his nose pressing it to the window whenever he heard a car come up the long driveway to the villa.

But no, each time he'd been bitterly disappointed. He hadn't shown it on his face, but for years that disappointment had burned and festered inside him like a fetid sore. One conversation with Daisy and it had all come bubbling to the surface. How much more would she get out of him if he let her too close?

He had watched his older brother painfully struggle

to keep the family together, taking on responsibilities that no child of ten should ever have to shoulder.

He had seen his strong and capable father reduced to a skin-wrapped skeleton in a chair, wearing nappies like a baby. The indignity of it had been stomach-churning. The suffering of his father had been like a brooding presence in the villa—haunting, maudlin, tortured.

From as young as he could remember, Luiz had chosen to enjoy life in the fast lane because he knew how quickly things could change. He pushed the limits but only as far as he knew he could go. The adrenalin rush of a new challenge energised him. Hadn't that been the most alluring thing about Daisy? She hadn't fallen at his feet as he'd expected. Even now she wasn't playing by his rules.

What would happen if he dared to relax them just this once?

CHAPTER FIVE

'OF COURSE, IF you don't think you're up to the task of taking me on then I'm sure I'll soon find some other guy to—' Daisy began.

'No, you won't.' Luiz's tone was strident. 'From what I've seen so far, you'll probably pick up some sleazy creep who'll take more than your virginity off you. Your credit card details, for instance. Or your passport. No wonder your old man won't let you out alone. Do you have any idea of the danger you could get into in a place like this?'

Daisy was finding his protective streak rather endearing. Underneath that suave and sophisticated über-modern exterior he was as old-fashioned as her father. Which was why she wanted him to be the one to make love to her for the first time. He ticked all the boxes for a holiday fling. He was gorgeous and fun-loving. He was respectably dissolute—a bad boy from a good family. He wouldn't make demands on her past the time frame of their fling. Who could be better to give her the experience she longed for than a man who was a professional playboy? It wasn't as if she was in any danger of falling in love with him. He was the total opposite of what she wanted in a long-term partner.

Besides, Belinda was always ragging her for not stepping outside her comfort zone. A red-hot fling with world champion polo player Luiz Valquez would win her some serious bragging rights.

Not to mention she was *seriously* attracted to him.

Daisy smiled up at him. 'So you'll do it?'

He was glowering as if she'd asked him to skin a spider before swallowing it. 'Aren't you being a little cold-blooded about this?'

'What's wrong? Surely you don't expect me to wrap it up in flowery language? I bet you don't when you select your next sleepover partner.'

He stalked to the other side of the room, one of his hands rubbing at the back of his neck as if he had a knot of tension bothering him. 'This is crazy. I can't believe I'm having this conversation.'

'Is it because I'm not a supermodel? I've heard you're really picky over your partners.'

'Not picky enough, it seems,' he muttered not quite under his breath.

'Yes, well, now that you mention it, you were the one who started this by approaching me in the nightclub,' she said. 'Who knows? If you hadn't been so full of yourself I mightn't have gone off with the Ealing guy and then none of this would have happened.'

His top lip curled. 'Is that your version of logic? If so, it's a little short of the mark.'

Daisy gave a small shrug. 'I'm just saying…'

He came back over to her, standing right in front of

her so she had to crane her neck to keep eye contact. His eyes moved between both of hers, back and forth, as if he were waiting for her to reveal some other motive other than pure unadulterated lust. After a moment he lifted his hand and stroked his fingertip across her jawline. His touch was mesmerising, light as air, and yet every nerve of hers twanged with awareness. 'I should send you packing.'

'That would be the sensible thing to do if I had indeed anything to pack before I left,' Daisy said. 'I don't suppose visiting the Grand Canyon in a little black dress and heels is sensible either.'

His half smile made her stomach slip. So did his touch as he cupped her cheek in one of his broad hands. His thumb moved over her cheek in a stroking motion that was as hypnotic as his dark chocolate gaze. 'No. It isn't.'

Daisy looked at his mouth, wondering if he was going to kiss her again. Never had a kiss been so exciting. Every pore of her body had responded to him. It was as if he had turned a switch on inside her body. Her inner core pulsated with the need to feel his thick male presence—a real flesh and blood man, not a cold and clinical machine. She could feel the twitching of those delicate nerves in anticipation of his intimate invasion. 'Maybe I should head back to my hotel and slip into something a little more touristy.'

'You should.'

She looked at the way his eyes became sleepily hooded, the dark fan of his lashes shielding half of his gaze as it focused on her mouth. 'Should I bring my things back here, do you think?'

His eyes sprang open again. 'What for?'

'Well, if we're going to hang out together for the next four days it would make sense, wouldn't it?'

He frowned as if he hadn't considered that angle before. 'How far away is your hotel?'

'It's down the budget end of the strip. It's what the girls could afford.' Daisy nibbled at her lip before adding, 'I guess I could cab it back and forth...'

'And make me look like a tight-fisted jerk?' he said. 'No. You can move in here with me.'

'Are you sure?'

'I'm not sleeping over in some flea-bitten dive.'

'It's not *that* far down the strip,' Daisy said. 'Mind you, this place must cost a packet. Do you always stay on the penthouse floor?'

'I like my space.'

'For all your wild parties?'

He gave her a stern look. 'I'm a professional sportsman. If I partied as hard as everyone made out in the press I wouldn't be able to win a single game.'

She angled her head as she surveyed his frowning expression. 'And winning is everything to you, isn't it?'

'I don't play polo to lose.'

'What about life?'

'That too.'

Daisy acknowledged that with a thoughtful nod. 'Which is why you don't invest in relationships, right?'

His lip curled mockingly again. 'Is the psychoanalysis part of the deal or is that a bonus?'

Daisy ignored his sarcasm as she tilted her head like a dealer assessing a unique work of art. 'You love your brother and you loved your father, but you hold your mother at arm's length, as you do all women. Your relationship with her is on your terms, not hers. You have attachment issues. Textbook case, in my opinion.'

Two lines of tension ran from his nose to his mouth. 'If you want your four days of fun then maybe you should keep your opinions to yourself.'

'Fair enough.'

His brow was deeply furrowed. 'That's it?'

'What?'

'You're going to do what you're told?'

Daisy gave him an innocent-as-pie look. 'Sure. That's what you want, isn't it? You only sleep with women who don't stand up to you—correct? They're not allowed to have a mind or opinions of their own. You just want their body, not their intellect. I can do that. Mind you, four days is about my limit, though.'

He let out another curse as he thrust a hand through the thickness of his hair. 'You are un-effing-believable.'

The sound of his phone ringing from the desk where he'd left it broke the silence. Daisy watched as he snatched it up and barked out a curt greeting. She couldn't hear the conversation but his expression went from dark and stormy to a slowly spreading smile that made the corners of his eyes crinkle attractively.

He ended the call and slipped his phone in his trouser pocket, sending her a glinting look. 'It seems there might be some fringe benefits for me in this crazy scheme of yours after all.'

'Oh?'

'That was one of the big time sponsors I've been chasing for months. He wouldn't play ball. Until now.'

'Why now?'

Luiz took her hand and entwined his fingers with hers, drawing her a step closer to his tall hard frame. 'Because up until now he thought I was a reckless playboy who would bring nothing but disrepute to his precious company's name. But a tweet's just gone out about us being a couple.'

Daisy could feel the electric zing of his touch racing all the way to her armpit and beyond. 'You mean he'll back you now? Because of me?'

His eyes shone with triumph. 'Apparently one of his goddaughters goes to your school. She's not in your class but he's heard nothing but praise for you. He figures if you're involved with me then I must be worth backing. This is exactly what I need to win the Argentine Open Championship.'

'Why do you need his sponsorship? Don't you have plenty of money of your own?'

'It's not about the money,' he said. 'It's the show of confidence in my ability I'm after. Look at the top sportsmen and women in golf and tennis or skiing or snowboarding or whatever. Their sponsors build their image. They brand it. The better your brand, the more confidence people have in your talent. That show of confidence boosts your own. It feeds off it.'

Daisy was pleased for him but she could see the pitfalls even if he couldn't. 'What are you going to say to your sponsor when we break up at the end of the week?'

She could almost see the cogs of his brain ticking over. His triumphant expression faltered momentarily before he beamed her a confident smile. 'We can always extend our fling. It's only a month till the Grand Slam.'

Daisy frowned at him. 'Aren't you forgetting something? I live in London. I have a job to go to. I'm only here now because the girls wanted me to come to Vegas with them for half-term break.'

'The Argentine Open is on the first Saturday in December,' he said. 'I could fly you over for it.'

It sounded wonderfully exotic. A trip to Buenos Aires, all expenses paid. A box seat to see one of the most talented polo players in the world battle it out for the ultimate crown. It would be something to remember when she was just another suburban wife and mother trying to juggle work and family.

'But what about the other three weeks?' she asked.

'The sponsor is based in London so I'll be back and forth,' he said. 'We can meet up often enough to keep the press from thinking anything's amiss.'

Daisy ignored the red flag that warned against spending too much time with the wickedly charming Luiz Valquez. She had asked for four days and now she had the chance to have four weeks. She'd wanted a walk on the wild side, hadn't she? This was her chance to make it one to remember. 'OK. You're on.'

He took her by the shoulders and pressed a blisteringly hot kiss to her mouth. Daisy leaned into him, unable to help herself from responding with burgeoning passion. He only had to touch her and she erupted into flames. She could feel the heat rushing through her veins, sending electric sensations through every cell in her body.

His hands cupped her face, his fingers splaying out over her cheeks as he deepened the kiss. His tongue played cat and mouse with hers, teasing and taunting hers to fight back. She flicked her tongue against his, doing her own little teasing routine, delighting in the way he groaned in the back of his throat and brought his pelvis hard against hers. She felt the hard ridge of him, the pressure of his blood building as his desire for her escalated. She stroked her hands down over the taut curve of his buttocks, bringing him in closer so she could feel the imprint of his erect flesh on hers.

His hands left her face; one went to her left hip, the other to the zip at the back of her dress. He rolled it down, exposing her spine from the base of her neck to the crease at the top of her bottom. He slid his hand over her skin, discovering every one of her vertebrae in turn. His touch evoked a delicious shower of reaction, especially when he came to the curve of her bottom. She immediately tensed her buttocks, hoping he wouldn't think her fat.

'Relax for me, *querida*,' he whispered against the skin of her neck.

'I'm not good at getting naked with people.'

He sent his tongue over her top lip and then her bottom one in a barely-there caress that made her lips sing with delight. 'You were pretty relaxed about it last night.'

Did he have to remind her? 'Yes, well, I was apparently off my face, which would have helped.'

He eased back to look at her with a slight frown. 'You're embarrassed about your body?'

What was he implying? That she had something to *be* embarrassed about? The cruel chant of one of the mean girls at boarding school rang in her ears: 'Lazy Daisy… Fat Daisy'. Not a natural sportsperson, Daisy had used every excuse in the book to avoid playing team sport. A sudden increase in weight during puberty had made her ashamed of her body, a shame she had never been able to shed. Even though she was more or less average weight for her height and build, there was still a mean girl's voice in her head that taunted her every time she stepped in front of a mirror. 'Let's put it this way. The only catwalk I've been anywhere near is my neighbour's moggie stalking a bird in the garden.'

There was a smile in his eyes as he slid his hand underneath her knickers, exploring her curves with the warm palm of his hand. 'Did he catch it?'

'The bird? No, I stepped in before it got to bloodshed.'

Still holding her gaze, he sent his finger down the crease of her bottom, a shamefully erotic caress that triggered a firestorm in her core. 'You have a beautiful body.'

'I wonder how many times you've used that line.'

His slight frown reappeared. 'I mean it, *querida.* You have a womanly figure. Curves in all the right places.'

'My breasts are too small.'

'Says who?'

Daisy felt a rush of heat as his gaze went to the modest cleavage he uncovered as he slipped her dress from her shoulders. She stopped breathing altogether when he slowly traced his finger over each upper curve of her breasts that were pushed up by her lacy bra. He touched her nipples through the lace, which somehow intensified the sensation. The lace abrading her erect flesh made something deep and low in her belly roll over.

'So beautiful.' He brought his mouth to her right breast, kissing the cupped flesh until she was writhing with the pleasure of it. He did the same to the other one, stroking his tongue over the exposed curve. Her breasts were tingling all over. She could feel them swelling inside the cage of her bra, peaking against the lace cups as if desperate to get out so they could feel his mouth and lips and tongue directly.

As if reading her mind, he deftly unhooked her bra and it fell to the floor along with her dress. She was standing in nothing but her knickers and her heels and for once in her life she couldn't give a damn. He made her feel beautiful with his dark lustrous eyes roving over her form as if he wanted to eat her alive. Everywhere his gaze rested burned and tingled. Everywhere his hands touched made her flesh shiver and dance in delight.

But she couldn't have him doing all the touching and caressing.

Daisy wanted to touch and caress him. To devour him. She started on the buttons of his shirt, undoing them one by one, leaning into him to press a kiss to the hot musky satin of his skin. She used her tongue to anoint him. Little stabs. Little flicks. Little licks. Feeling thrilled as he sucked in a breath as if her ministrations excited him like no other.

She slid her hands over his rock-hard pectoral muscles, exploring his flat male nipples with her fingertips, pressing a moist kiss to each one, following it up with a hot swirl of her tongue.

'You're a dangerous woman,' he growled against her neck, taking a nip of her sensitive skin like a wolf did to control an overly amorous mate.

Daisy felt something wild and primitive inside her break free. She stepped up on tiptoe and put her mouth to his neck, taking a section of his flesh and biting down just hard enough to feel the tension of his skin. She released it to sweep her tongue over the spot, lulling him into a false sense of security before she bit him again.

He swore playfully and came back at her with a bite on her breast that was just shy of painful. Pleasure exploded like firecrackers under her skin.

But he wasn't done yet.

He sucked her nipple into his mouth. Gently pulling on it with his hot wet mouth, drawing on it until she was hovering in that tantalising place somewhere between pleasure and pain. He moved to her other nipple, rolling his tongue over it, circling it, teasing it, and then gently sinking his teeth just enough to pinch the flesh.

Daisy pressed her burning pelvis against the scorching heat of his. Rampant need was crawling all over her skin, making her breathless and mindless in her pursuit of ultimate pleasure. Never had her body felt more electrically alive. Never had it ached with such relentless want. Never had she been so desperate to come apart. The tension was like a pressure cooker inside her body. Building. Building. Building.

He slid his hands back over her buttocks, cupping her to his body, letting her feel the outline of his arousal. 'I want you.'

'I want you too.'

He walked her back towards the nearest wall, hooking his fingers into her knickers, but somehow in the haste to get them off his fingers tore through the fine cobweb of lace. He glanced at them ruefully, a frown pulling at his brow. 'Sorry.'

'It's fine.' Daisy kicked them away with her foot. 'Now, where were we? Oh, I remember. We were doing something about all these clothes you're wearing.'

She proceeded to tug the tail of his shirt out of his trousers. But suddenly his hands came down and stalled her. 'Wait,' he said, breathing heavily.

She raised her brows in surprise. 'What for?'

He stepped back from her and pushed one of his hands through his hair. His gaze went back to the tiny scrap of torn lace on the floor at his feet, his brow furrowing tighter as he bent down to pick them up. He handed them to her, his expression now inscrutable. 'I'll buy you a new pair.'

What did she care about a silly little pair of chain store knickers when her body was screaming for release? But then a host of self-doubts flooded her system. It was like throwing a bucket of ice cubes on her nascent sexual confidence. She wasn't like his usual conquests. She wasn't catwalk-skinny. She wasn't beautiful enough for the likes of him. She gathered what remnants of pride she could and set about getting back into her dress and bra, all the while conscious of him silently watching her, still with that unreadable expression on his face.

'Was it something I said?' she asked after a painful silence.

'No.'

'Something I did?'

'No.'

'Something I didn't?'

'No.'

Daisy pushed her lips out on an expelled breath as she smoothed down her dress. 'You really know how to leave a girl hanging.'

'I'm sorry.' His hand went through his hair again, this time from front to back, leaving it all sexily tousled as if he'd just got out of bed. 'I'm not used to doing things this way.'

'Which way is that? We're both adults who are attracted to each other. What other way are you talking about?'

He drew in an audible breath before slowly releasing it. 'You're a virgin, for one thing.'

Daisy wrinkled her brow in a frown. 'What's that got to do with it?'

'Having sex for the first time can be an intensely emotional experience.'

'Was it for you?'

He frowned as if the thought was ludicrous. 'No, not at all.'

'So why should it be intensely emotional for me?'

He looked at her for a moment without speaking, his eyes surveying every feature on her face as if she was a complicated puzzle he couldn't quite figure out. 'It's different for women. It's harder for them to separate their emotions from the physicality of sex. Especially the first time.'

'How many virgins have you slept with?'

'None that I know of.'

'So how can you speak with such authority?'

He let out another long breath. 'Look, I don't want you to get hurt, OK? You're a good girl, and in my experience good girls and bad boys don't mix.'

Daisy wasn't sure what he was saying. Was he saying their fling wasn't going to go ahead after all? Disappointment felt like a weary ache in her bones. 'So what happens now?'

He rubbed at his shadowed jaw before dropping his hand by his side. 'We'll hang out together as planned.'

'And what about sex?'

'I think it's best if we leave sex out of it.'

Daisy blinked. 'No sex?'

A tiny muscle beat a one-two rhythm at the side of his mouth. 'No sex.'

She ran her tongue over her lips, wondering why he was suddenly baulking at the idea of becoming intimate with her. Surely this wasn't just about her looks. He had been as turned on as her just moments ago. She had seen and felt the evidence with her own eyes and hands. Was it the thought of the time frame that was putting him off? He was used to one-night stands. He didn't have relationships with women. He had hook-ups. Quick, temporary transactions that involved their bodies, not their minds or their emotions or, indeed, his. 'So, let me get this straight… You want me to *pretend* to be your lover until after the Grand Slam but we're not going to have sex?'

'Correct.'

'Will we kiss?'

The muscle near his mouth started beating again. 'If the occasion demands it.'

'What occasion might that be?'

'A public one.'

'Oh, right. Silly me. I thought maybe you'd want to kiss me because you found me irresistibly attractive and just couldn't help yourself.' She scooped her purse off the coffee table and slipped her knickers inside and clipped it shut. 'Let's not forget *you* were the one to give me the biggest come-on in the nightclub.'

'I'm doing this for you, Daisy.'

She clutched a hand to her heart theatrically. 'For *me?* How incredibly sweet.'

He gave her a black look. 'Don't be like that.'

She pressed her lips tightly together as she studied him. 'Is this because of my father?'

'He's got a right to be worried about you. You're a loose cannon.'

Daisy decided right then and there she would show him just how loose she could be. He might want to keep things on a platonic level but she had other ideas. She wanted her holiday fling and she wanted it with him and no one—not even his newly invented moral code—was going to stop her. 'I'm going back to my hotel to get my things.'

He reached for his room key. 'I'll come with you. The press will be—'

'No, don't do that. I'll meet you back here in ten or fifteen minutes.'

A frown was beetling his brows. 'I might as well come with you and wait until you're ready.'

'Erm, I don't think so.' She gave him a cryptic little smile. 'Edward might not like that.'

His frown deepened. 'Who the hell…? Oh…'

Daisy lifted her hand in a cheery fingertip wave. 'See you in fifteen.'

CHAPTER SIX

LUIZ CAUGHT HER before she got into the elevator. Thankfully, the press had moved on now they had their story. And what a story it was. How had he ended up in this melodrama? One act of chivalry and he was in so deep he didn't know whether he was coming or going. Well, he definitely hadn't come, but it had been a close shave. Closer than he cared to admit.

The shock of seeing that torn scrap of lace had reminded him of what he'd been about to do. Deflowering virgins, even ones with attitude, was not on his agenda. Especially ones with fathers with agendas of their own. He had to do the right thing by her and not just because of her old man. She was a nice kid. A bit ditzy and naïve, but in a way that was what was so darned refreshing about her. She didn't treat him as if he was a demigod. She hadn't even known who he was when she'd first met him. It was only his protection of her that had changed her mind about him.

Now she had her mind set on him being her first lover…apart from her mechanical boyfriend, that was. He might be a thoroughly modern guy and chilled about all things sexual, but there was no way he was going to stand outside the door and let some battery-operated device do what he ached and throbbed to do. If he had to be celibate for the next couple of weeks, then Daisy could damn well join him.

He slipped in before the elevator doors closed and faced her squarely. 'You can't go haring off by yourself. We're supposed to be a couple. Couples do everything together.' *Or so I'm told.*

Her bright blue eyes with their dark fan of lashes looked up at him guilelessly. 'But the press have gone now.'

'That's not the point.' He reached over to stab at the ground floor button as if it had personally insulted him. 'There are people with camera phones everywhere. One shot of one of us without the other and the gossip will start. There'll be speculation that we're over. I can't afford to let that happen until the paperwork is secure on my sponsorship.'

'Fine, I'll stick to you like glue.' She closed the distance between them and looped an arm through his. 'I'll be your little shadow.'

Little tormentor, more like, Luiz thought, as the soft skin of her arm brushed against the hairs on his. He looked at her mouth, that delicious curve that was always on the verge of smiling, the cute little dimples that appeared when she did.

How had she lasted this long without someone snapping her up? She was gorgeous and super sexy and she kissed with such passion his body was still thrumming with the aftershocks.

How was he going to keep his hands off her for the duration of their 'relationship'? The sensation of her soft creamy breasts against his mouth, the way her tender skin caught against his stubble, the feel of her tightly budded nipples against his tongue and the soft little gasp she gave with each of his caresses made his body writhe with sexual hunger.

He would have to fly in icy water from Antarctica to douse the heat she had stirred in his blood.

'Stop looking at me like that,' he growled.

'How am I looking at you?'

He put his hands on her shoulders and turned her so she was facing the mirrored panel on the elevator. 'Like that.'

She leaned back against him, the sexy cheeks of her bottom brushing against his still swollen erection. There was a secret smile playing about her mouth and her sparkling eyes were full of mischief. 'Like this?'

Luiz's hands slipped down to hold her hips. His rational brain said, *No! Don't do it!* But his body was acting of its own volition. His blood ran hot and urgent with the need to press against her. Her light and delicate fragrance wafted past his nostrils—cottage flowers this time, with the alluring and exotic grace notes of sun-warmed honeysuckle. Her lips were without lipgloss or lipstick but they were as red as spring's first rose. Her complexion had not a single blemish. Not even a freckle. He had never seen skin so pure and untainted. The comparison with his was stark. His was olive-toned and tanned from a lifetime of playing polo and other outdoor sports.

His hand moved up to sit just below her right breast. He could feel the slight weight of it resting against the line of his thumb. She brought one of her hands over his, her small, slim fingers looking as small and dainty as a child's compared to his. She danced her fingers over the back of his hand, and then started toying with the coarse masculine hair that fanned from his hand and down each of his fingers.

'You have nice hands,' she said.

Luiz couldn't help himself. His hand came up and settled over her breast, her tight little nipple pressing against his palm. He heard her draw in a breath, saw the flash of pleasure on her face. Felt the thunderous roar of his lust charging through his body like a wild bull on a stampede.

He spun her around and brought his mouth down to hers in a crushing kiss, heat exploding like a volcano as his tongue found hers. The hot, sweet wetness of her mouth made his longing for her body all the more intense. He could feel his erection straining against the zip on his trousers. He pulled her as close to him as it was possible to be while still clothed. Her breasts were jammed against his chest, her hips flush with his, her thighs tangling with his in a desperate attempt to get even closer. She made soft little mewling sounds of approval in her throat, her arms snaking up around his neck, her clever little fingers spreading through his hair, tugging and pulling and caressing.

He could feel the scrape of his stubble along her skin as he shifted position, reminding him again of her softness against his hardness. His tongue found hers again, coiled around it, danced with it, taunted and teased it until it finally gave in to his command.

He sucked on her lower lip, and then he used his teeth to nip and tug at the tender flesh, following it up with a sweep of his tongue and then repeating the process.

Her tongue flicked against his, a sexy little payback that heated his blood to sizzling. Her teeth got into the action, biting him like a tigress did an aggressive mate, showing him she was not going to submit without a fight.

Luiz had never experienced a more enthralling kiss. His whole body was feeling the supercharge of it. Nerve endings were firing in his lips, sensations were racing up and down his spine, and his thighs were trembling with the pressure of holding himself in. He knew if she so much as put her hand on him he would blow.

The doors of the elevator sprang open and he had a deer-in-the-headlights moment as a camera flashed in his face. He smothered a rough curse and dropped his hands from Daisy's hips.

'Get a room!' someone jeered.

Luiz grabbed Daisy's hand and pulled her behind him. 'Let's get out of here.'

Daisy was bundled into a limousine within seconds of leaving Luiz's hotel. He was still holding her hand, his long calloused fingers wrapped around hers in a bruising grip. High on his aristocratic cheekbones two flags of dull colour were showing beneath his tan. His coal-black eyes were fixed straight ahead but she had a feeling he wasn't registering any of the lurid colour and excitement and craziness of the strip as they traversed the length of it.

'Are you angry with me?' she asked.

He glanced at her as if he had forgotten she was there. 'No. Why do you ask that?'

She indicated her hand trapped within his. 'You're cutting off my circulation.'

He immediately relaxed his hold but he didn't release her hand. Rather he began to caress it in slow, soothing strokes. 'I'm sorry. I didn't realise.'

Daisy looked at his brooding expression. 'Do the press follow you everywhere?'

'Just about.'

'Don't you find it...annoying?'

'Sometimes.'

She moved her fingers over the length of his index finger, circling each of his knuckles and then the neat square of his fingernail. 'Why don't you do something about it?'

He glanced down at her. 'Like what?'

'You could wear a disguise.'

He gave a short laugh. 'As if that would work.'

'A lot of celebrities do it. You'd be surprised how effective it is. A wig or a hat or a different style of clothes can make all the difference. When my kindy kids get in the dress-up box it's impossible to tell who is who. Sometimes even their parents don't recognise them.'

He looked back at their joined hands, his thumb moving over the back of hers in a rhythmic fashion. 'It bothers my brother more than it does me. I guess I'm like my mother in that regard. I've never shied away from the limelight.'

'What's your brother like?'

His thumb found the heel of her hand and began to massage it. 'He's strong. Determined. Focused.'

'Like you, then.'

He smiled a half-smile. 'I'm not sure he would agree with you on that.'

'Why?'

'He doesn't say it upfront, but he thinks I'm chasing a dream that will only disappoint in the end.'

'The Championship?'

He met her gaze again. 'Winning is everything to me. It's always been my main motivation. Being the best.'

'I guess what your brother's saying is one day someone will come along who's better than you,' Daisy said. 'You can't win for ever.'

His gaze went to her mouth. 'No, but I like to think I'll know when it's time to hang up my hat.'

'You mean go out on a high?'

His eyes searched hers for a long moment. 'Did you always want to be a teacher?'

Daisy grinned. 'Always. I used to line up my dolls when I was about three or so and play schools with them for hours.'

There was a serious light in his gaze. 'Did you have a happy childhood?'

Her smile faded as she thought about her mother's restlessness and her father's controlling ways. 'In the early days, but then my mum's accident changed everything. She died when I was ten. A car ran into her as she was coming home from bridge club. My father was always a bit of a control freak but after that he was unbelievable. I couldn't go anywhere without a nanny or babysitter. I had heaps of them over the years. Dad would always upset them over something and they'd storm out in tears. Fear does terrible things to people, doesn't it?'

He gave her hand an absent squeeze. 'Yes, indeed it does.'

Daisy glanced out of the window as her hotel came into view. 'Oh, look. The girls are waiting for me outside. I texted them while I was waiting for the elevator.'

'What did you tell them?'

She gave them a mad wave. 'The truth.'

'Which version?' His tone was dry. 'I'm having a little trouble keeping up.'

Daisy looked at him again. 'Oh, they know I'm not really in love with you. That would be taking things to ridiculous extremes.'

His expression was deadpan. 'Quite.'

'But they're the ones—Belinda in particular—who encouraged me to put myself out there and find myself a holiday romance.' She grinned at him. 'How lucky am I? I asked for four days and you're giving me four weeks. Cool, huh?'

His smile looked a little tight. 'Way cool.'

Luiz stood back as Daisy was reunited with her friends. There was a group hug and lots of excited chatter and a few sideways glances in his direction and some nudging and winking. He took it in good spirit because he wasn't going to risk his sponsorship deal before it even got off the ground. Once it was done and dusted he could distance himself from the engaging Miss Daisy before she drove him crazy. The more time he spent with her, the more he wanted her. Now he had four weeks with her. *Four weeks!* He had trouble being celibate for four hours, let alone four weeks. Once they parted in Vegas he would keep things to a minimum. He could take her out to dinner in London but he wouldn't stay with her or have her stay with him. That would be testing his resolve a little too far. If he kept their dates public he would be home free.

While Daisy was collecting her things, Luiz organised a helicopter for the Grand Canyon. He figured a day outside in the fresh air was another good way to distract himself from the temptation of taking her to bed.

Once they were on their way in the limousine he told her what he had planned. 'We'll fly over Hoover Dam first and then on to the Grand Canyon. You'll get a good view of both.'

'Oh, lovely,' she said. 'But you shouldn't have gone to any trouble.'

'It's no trouble.'

'But what did you have planned for today?'

Luiz wasn't used to his dates being concerned about him, only what he could do for them. Daisy's concern was not only refreshing but it was surprisingly genuine. Her blue eyes had a worried light in them as she waited for his reply.

'Nothing much,' he said. 'A bit of time in the gym, a few games of poker. Chilling out.'

'So is that why you're here in Vegas now? Just for a holiday?'

Why did he go anywhere when he wasn't competing? To distract himself from moping around his huge empty villa in Argentina. If he didn't fill his spare time with parties and people he got restless and bored. His older brother enjoyed solitude. Luiz didn't. Time alone reminded him too much of how he had felt as a child.

Abandoned.

'I come over a couple of times a year. It's a great place to blend into the crowd.' He realised too late the irony of what he'd just said and sent her a wry smile. 'Well, maybe not always.'

She gave him a sympathetic look. 'I'd hate to be famous. It must be awful to have cameras thrust in your face all the time. Never being able to go anywhere without someone tailing you.'

'Having a bodyguard must be similar.'

She rolled her eyes. 'Tell me about it.'

Luiz glanced out of the back window of the limousine. 'Is he still following you?'

'No. I called my father when I was packing my things and made him promise. I think he finally accepts I'm safe with you.'

You're not safe, he thought. *But then, I'm not safe either. Damn it.*

The helicopter was waiting for them when they arrived. Luiz handed Daisy the headset and went through the safety features.

'But what about the pilot?' she asked.

He adjusted her earphones so they sat correctly. 'I'm your pilot.'

Her eyes rounded. 'You're a pilot?'

He couldn't help touching her chin where the red mark from his stubble was still faintly apparent. 'Got my licence years ago.'

Her eyes began to sparkle. 'Do you have any other secret talents I should know about?'

'None that I can show you right now.' Do *not* flirt with her. Do. Not. Flirt. With. Her.

Her smile had a touch of naughty girl about it. 'I bet you have lots of tricks up your sleeve.'

Right now my biggest trick is not up my sleeve, Luiz thought as he helped her into the passenger seat. His hand inadvertently brushed against her breast as he pulled the seat belt into place.

Her eyes met his in a little lock that made his blood hurtle through his veins. Her eyes had tiny flecks of slate in amongst the intense blue, reminding him of an ocean with hidden depths. Her lashes were spider leg long and spiky with a coat of mascara. The point of her tongue darted out to sweep over her lips, making it impossible for him not to stare at the soft shiny lushness of her mouth.

He brought his mouth closer, pausing within a whisker of her slightly parted lips. Her sweet cinnamon and honey breath danced over the surface of his lips, her signature fragrance of old-fashioned cottage flowers teasing his senses into an intoxicated stupor.

'Is someone watching?' she said.

'Not that I know of.' He nudged his nose against hers. 'Why?'

'You're about to kiss me.'

'So?'

'So I thought someone must be watching.'

He couldn't pull himself away from the lure of her soft mouth that tantalisingly brushed against his lower lip every time she spoke. 'Can't I kiss you when no one's watching?'

'Sure. But I thought—'

'Stop thinking.' Luiz wasn't sure if he was saying it to her or himself. 'Just feel.'

He closed the distance between their mouths with a soft press against hers but as soon as her mouth flowered open he was gone. He drove his tongue into her mouth to meet hers; tangling with it in a passionate duel that made the base of his spine shudder and his groin fill with pulsating blood.

Her hands came up to cradle his face, a tender gesture that was at odds with the heated fervour of her kiss. But that was the complexity of her—the beguiling mix of passion and innocence that so knocked him off kilter.

He encircled her wrists with his hands, reluctantly pulling away before things got too out of hand. He needed to stay in control. It was what he did best. He pushed the boundaries as far as he could but no further. He knew his limits and Daisy Wyndham was testing every damn one of them.

She looked at him with a quizzical expression, her mouth all soft and glistening from his moistness and hers. 'Is something wrong?'

Before he could stop himself, he gently brushed her cheek with his index finger. 'We should get going. I've only booked this helicopter for a couple of hours.'

'Oh…right, of course.' She settled back in her seat, wriggling her shoulders and testing the strength of the seat belt, a little frown pulling at her smooth brow.

Luiz brought her chin around so her gaze met his. 'You're safe with me, *querida.*'

Her blue eyes were as clear and pure as a mountain stream. 'But what if I don't want to be?'

CHAPTER SEVEN

IT WAS A breathtaking experience, winging over the engineering marvel of Hoover Dam, but it was nothing to the vista of the magnificent Grand Canyon a short while later. The majestic height of the layers of richly coloured sandstone, the seemingly endless sinuous curve of the Colorado River so far below and the wheeling of a lonely bird of prey and the whistling silence was such a stunning contrast to the madcap noise and frenetic activity of Las Vegas.

Luiz pointed out various landmarks to Daisy, such as Eagle Point, the Grand Canyon Skywalk and Guano Point, telling her some of the history of the first people, the Hualapai tribe. But, rather than land amongst all the tourist buses and cars, he flew her to a quiet gorge where he'd organised special permission to land.

Daisy held her breath in wonder as he brought the helicopter down the face of the canyon into a deep shaded gully where the river flowed as it had done for millions of years. Once the helicopter engine had turned off and the whirling blades ceased, the sense of timelessness struck her as she stood with Luiz in the cool green valley between the huge rock walls of the canyon. The lonely cry of a red-tailed hawk added to the sense of peace and serenity. She didn't want to speak for fear of breaking the spell of mystical silence.

Luiz stood shoulder to shoulder with her. He didn't speak either. He just stood there with a hand shading his eyes as he surveyed their surroundings.

She stole covert glances at him from time to time, watching as he bent down to pick up a little piece of sandstone, turning it over in his fingers before tossing it in the direction of the river, where the *plop* of the pebble as it went down sounded as loud as a rifle shot.

Daisy sensed a deep loneliness in him. He was so popular, so capable, so much the man about town, but out here in the quiet of the timeless canyon he reminded her of one of the birds of prey circling overhead. Solitary. Alone.

Without a word he led her back to the helicopter, guiding her back into her seat and helping her with the headset. She studied his concentrated expression, wondering what he was thinking as he got back behind the controls for take-off. His hands dealt with the controls with the expertise of a pro. He was as at home in the cockpit as he was working the floor at a nightclub or working his way around a woman's body. She hadn't seen him live on horseback but she had looked at some footage online on her phone. He was a natural sportsman, athletic, strong, capable and fiercely competitive.

She glanced at his strongly muscled thighs, so close

to hers in the cockpit. She only had to reach out her hand to touch him. Her fingers opened and closed, warming up for the first caress of that denim-clad thigh.

'Not while I'm flying.'

Daisy looked at him in surprise. 'You knew what I was thinking?'

He glanced at her wryly. 'I thought you were a good girl?'

'Not when I'm with you.'

He made a grunting sound in his throat as he turned back to face the front. 'Fancy a swim when we get back to the hotel?'

Daisy pictured a private pool off his suite with a bubbling Jacuzzi and champagne in an ice bucket close at hand. Fragrant lotions and potions on tap for hours of sensual massage. She smiled a secret smile. Just as well Belinda had slipped her that racy little Brazilian-style bikini earlier. Body issues aside, her conservative one-piece would look totally out of place. It was time for her inner naughty girl to come out to play.

Luiz was keeping her at arm's length but she knew he wanted her. Every time he looked at her she felt the burn of his hungry gaze. She imagined how it would feel to make love on the deck by the pool in the bright sunshine, his hard body driving hers to paradise. She wanted to make love with him. Desperately. But not like all his other partners. She wanted to be different. To be someone he remembered with a special fondness. She wasn't asking for love. She didn't want to fall in love with someone like him. He was not part of her long-term plan. But she did want him to care enough about her to spend more than one night with her.

She smiled at him. 'Sounds wonderful.'

Luiz waited for Daisy to get changed once they got back to his hotel. He checked his emails on his phone. Scrolled through Twitter. Read a couple of blogs he had zero interest in—anything to distract himself from the thought of spending the next hour or two with her dressed in a swimsuit. But at least going downstairs to the public pool area would be his insurance policy. He could hardly make out with her with all the other hotel guests milling about. He looked up when she came out of the bathroom. She was wearing one of the hotel bathrobes tied neatly at the waist and it was far too big for her. It covered her from neck to ankle.

So far, so good.

'Ready?'

'Sure.'

She untied the waist and the white robe fell to a puddle at her feet. Luiz felt his jaw clang to the floor. The soft mounds of her breasts spilled out from behind two tiny triangles of fuchsia-pink. The triangle that covered her pubic area was even tinier, the strings that held it in place barely thicker than dental floss.

'You can't wear that!'

Her brow puckered. 'Why not?'

'Everyone will see your…er…assets.'

'But I thought we were swimming in your pool?'

'The one downstairs is bigger.'

She toyed with one of the strings on her bikini bottoms. 'I don't care if it's small. I'd rather stay up here. I don't like swimming with crowds of people.'

Luiz had to think on his feet and fast. 'There's way too much chlorine in this one. It'll ruin your bikini. It'll make the colour fade.'

'That's easily fixed.' She tugged at one of the strings holding her top in place. 'I won't wear it.'

He feasted his eyes on the creamy globes of her breasts with their twin points of rosy pink. He slid his gaze down to her slim waist, then to the tiny cave of her belly button. He snatched in a breath as she gave her bikini bottom ties a tug. The scrap of fabric fell away to reveal her feminine form. She was like a closed orchid, soft delicate petals folded together.

She came towards him with a swinging catwalk gait, her hips swaying, her beautiful breasts jiggling tantalisingly, her good-girl-turned-naughty smile on her mouth and dancing in her eyes. 'You sure you want to go downstairs and swim in that crowded pool with all those other people?'

He swallowed thickly as she looped her arms around his neck, pushing her naked breasts against his chest. Even through the cotton of his shirt he could feel her nipples poking him. Lust charged through his body with rocket-force speed. His hands were on her waist before his brain had even registered the command. His mouth came down and covered hers in an explosive kiss that made his spine tingle from top to base.

Her tongue met his in a frenzied dance, moistly coiling and retreating, stabbing and darting around his until he had to ruthlessly take charge. He thrust deeply into her mouth, swirling his tongue over every corner of her mouth until, with a breathless little gasp, she succumbed. She melted against him, hands threading through his hair, her mouth a soft yielding pliancy beneath his.

He stroked his hands down her body, skirting over her breasts, sliding down her hips and back up again. Her skin was as smooth as cream and as soft as satin, every inch of her so perfectly feminine his body throbbed with the need to possess her.

He slid his hands down over the curve of her bottom, cupping her to him, relishing the feel of her so close to the pulsating need of his body. He continued to kiss her, deeply, thoroughly, delighting in the feel of her lips and tongue wrangling with his.

Her teeth made a series of kitten nips against his, thrilling his blood to fever-pitch. He did the same to her, pulling and tugging her lower lip with his teeth, reminding her he was the one with the greater strength.

Her hands went to the buttons of his shirt, undoing them with fumbling haste as her mouth played with the skin of his neck, over his collarbone, and down his sternum.

She smoothed her hands over each part of his chest as she uncovered it, sliding over and stroking him until he was so worked up he was having trouble keeping control. His erection strained, tight and aching, against the prison of his jeans.

Once he had shrugged off his shirt, she started on

his waistband fastening, releasing it and sliding his zip down. He watched as she peeled back his underwear, her small white hand stroking his length with tentative shyness. He held his breath as she smoothed the pad of her finger over the bead of pre-ejaculatory moisture at his tip. Her caresses became bolder as she saw the way he was responding.

He put his hand over hers, halting her movements before he disgraced himself. 'I need a minute.'

'You need me,' she said. 'I need you. I want you.'

'I want you too.' There. He'd admitted it. What was the point of trying to pretend otherwise? He hadn't a hope of holding out. She was too distracting. Too engaging. Too everything.

'Then why are you stalling?'

The irony didn't escape him. When had he ever been concerned about going too fast? Normally he was all for the faster, the better. He didn't hang around too long in case his casual partners got any funny ideas about taking things more seriously.

He didn't do serious.

He was in it for fun, not for ever.

But something about Daisy made him think of taking his time, indulging in an affair that lasted longer than an orgasm. She was like a good wine. It would be a sin to scull a fine wine without lingering over the bouquet, tasting the subtle nuances and reflecting on the aftertaste.

But even a good wine lost its appeal over time. There was always another variety waiting in the wings. He was like his mother in that way, always on the lookout for something or someone more exciting.

Although right now there was nothing he could think of that was more exciting than having Daisy Wyndham naked in his arms. Her body was so nubile and feminine he wanted to lose himself in her delectable curves.

Luiz brought his mouth back down to within a breath of hers. 'I'm not stalling,' he said. 'I'm just warming up.'

'So what was that about only kissing in public?'

Yeah, what was that? His attempt to control a situation that was never going to be in his control.

'I've changed my mind.'

He walked her backwards to the bed, his mouth locked on hers, their tongues duelling, their bodies straining to get as close as humanly possible. He quickly shucked off his jeans and shoes and socks and joined her on the bed. 'I don't want to hurt you.'

'How will you hurt me?'

He brushed a strand of hair away from her face, looking into the clear blue of her gaze. 'The first time can be painful.'

She gave him a twinkling look. 'Well, you *are* a little bigger than Edward.'

He pressed a hard kiss to her mouth. 'Wicked girl.'

She grinned at him. 'I'm learning.'

He brought his mouth to her breast, suckling at the tight nipple while she expressed her pleasure in little moans and gasps. He took his mouth further down her body, lingering over her belly button, dipping his tongue in and out before going lower. He traced the seam of her body with the tip of his tongue, once, twice, the third time gently opening her to taste her. She arched up in delight, her hands clutching at the bedcover either side of her. He felt her every tremble against his tongue, her breathless gasps like music to his ears. He varied his speed and pressure, encouraging her to relax into the rhythm of his caresses. She pulled back a couple of times as if shying away from the powerful sensations. He calmed her with slower movements, placing his hand on her belly, close to her mound to anchor her. She sighed deeply and he resumed his caresses, feeling the exact moment when she lifted off. He watched the spasms of ecstasy play out on her face; the intimacy of watching someone having an orgasm had never really struck him quite that way before. She was so open and free, so uninhibited, so perfectly natural it made his breath catch.

She opened her eyes and looked at him with a smile. 'It didn't hurt a bit.'

'Not yet, but it might.' Luiz took one of her hands and pressed a kiss to the middle of her palm. 'I'll take it slowly just in case.' He reached past her to retrieve a condom from the bedside drawer.

She turned her head to watch him. 'How many do you have in there?'

'Enough.'

'I suppose you buy them in the hundreds.'

He glanced at her to see if there was any sign of censure in her expression but, surprisingly, there was none.

Unless she was doing her best to disguise it, which was more likely. 'It's not good to hold on to them for too long. They have a use-by date.'

'Like your partners?'

He searched her gaze for another moment. 'Yes. Exactly like them.'

She trailed a fingertip down the length of his forearm. 'What's been your longest relationship?'

'Two weeks.'

Her brows lifted. 'That long?'

Luiz gave a rueful twist of his mouth. 'Yeah, it's a record. It was when I was a teenager. I fell madly in love at sixteen. She was a year older and had much more experience.'

'Who broke it off?'

'She did.'

'Ouch.'

He traced a slow circle on the back of her hand. 'She had a boyfriend she forgot to tell me about.' He met her gaze again. 'I was a fling to make him jealous.'

She frowned. 'That was pretty mean of her.'

'Quite.'

She lifted her hand to his face, stroking his lean cheek, her blue eyes holding his. 'So you've used women ever since.'

He pulled back from her hand and frowned. 'I don't use women.'

'Yes, you do. You hook up with them for sex. You don't spend any time getting to know them. If that's not using then I don't know what is.'

He pushed up off the bed and got to his feet, slamming the bedside drawer on the way. 'No one's complained so far.'

'No, because you buy them off with a flashy bit of jewellery or flowers.'

He sent her a cutting look. 'I see you and Mr Google have been getting up close and personal. What else have you found out about me?'

She sat up and hugged her knees to her chest, her teeth giving her lower lip a chew, her eyes now downcast. 'I think I just ruined the moment… Sorry.'

Luiz found it impossible to be angry with her. He let out a slow breath and came back to the bed and sat beside her. He took her hand and turned it over in his, playing with each of her fingers in turn. 'You don't approve of my lifestyle, do you?'

Her blue eyes were clear and open and honest as they met his. 'I don't know much about it, other than what I've read. You might have a completely different take on it. But one thing I do know. You can't live your whole life without connecting with other people on more than a physical level.'

He moved his thumb over the knuckle of hers in a slow motion caress. 'How come someone who's only had sex with a toy knows so much about connecting with people?'

Her cheeks blushed a faint pink. 'I've had sex with you…sort of…'

He watched as her gaze dropped to his mouth, her tongue sneaking out to moisten her lips in a darting sweep. He pressed the pad of his finger to her bottom lip, watching as the blood retreated and then flowed back in when he lifted it away. 'Want to pick up where we left off?'

He heard her draw in a quick little breath. 'Do you want to?'

He pressed her back down on the bed. 'Do I really need to answer that?'

She smiled as his body bore down on hers. 'I think you just did.'

CHAPTER EIGHT

DAISY SIGHED IN bliss as his mouth sealed hers in a searing kiss. His tongue stroked for entry in that commanding way he had, making her stomach turn over like a flipped pancake. His hand came down on her hip and pulled her up against him, one of his thighs coming over the top of hers in an intimate entrapment that made her skin pepper with goosebumps. His erection was pressed hard against her belly, a tantalising reminder of all the differences between them.

She reached down to stroke him, loving the feel of him pulsing with desire under her fingertips. He was oozing moisture and she felt her own beading inside her body in preparation for him.

One of his hands cupped her breast, his thumb pressing against her nipple, pushing it in and out, and then circling it. He bent his head to take it in his mouth, laving it with his tongue, tracing every inch of her flesh with soft but sure movements.

Daisy felt the rise of her need for him like a tremor before an earthquake. It moved through her flesh with every scorching touch of his mouth and hands on her body.

He rolled her over on her back, leaning his weight on his elbows. His mouth moved with erotic intent over hers, drawing from her a fevered response she hadn't realised she was capable of giving. She felt as if she would die if he didn't make love to her. She opened her legs and felt her stomach swoop as he settled between them. Somehow he'd managed to slip a condom on. She felt him at her entrance, hard, swollen, ready. She arched up to receive him, urging him to possess her without language but with unmitigated primal need.

He slowly entered her with a deep guttural groan of pleasure. Her body wrapped around him, holding him, delighting in him. Needing him like she needed air to breathe.

He steadily increased his pace, taking his time so she could find her own rhythm. She moved with him, lifting her hips to each of his downward thrusts, shuddering with pleasure as the friction targeted the most sensitive spot. The pleasure built to a crescendo. She could feel the tension in her body building like the overstretching of a violin string. Her body was singing, humming and thrumming with delicious shockwaves of feeling. A shiver coursed over her skin as he upped the pace, his thrusts deeper, harder and more frantic, as if he too was close to the summit of human pleasure.

He slipped one of his hands between their bodies to heighten the pleasure. It was all she needed to tip over the edge. The orgasm smashed into her in a giant wave that sent her flying higher than she had ever flown before. The combination of human touch, the musky fragrance of male arousal, the stroke and glide of clever hands and the expertise of his lips and tongue made a mockery of everything she had experienced on her own.

Daisy floated down from the heights with a rapturous sigh just in time to feel his release power through him. He tensed over her, poised in that nanosecond between control and freedom. He gave a primal growl and surged deep, shuddering his way through his orgasm, the skin on his back and shoulders rising in the fine gravel of goosebumps beneath her fingertips.

She heard him give a long, deep sigh before he collapsed on top of her, his head buried beside her neck, his breathing still racing.

It was so different being held in a man's arms. Being *wanted.* Her body was still tingling with the aftershocks of his possession. She hadn't expected it to be so utterly consuming. Her entire body had been swept away with the rushing sensations of pleasure. Was it because it was him, not some other man? Was it his experience or something else? Every step of the way he had made sure of her comfort and pleasure. He had taken extra care of her. How could that not have an impact on her reaction to him? He had made her first time not only special but also memorable. How would she ever forget this moment? He had taught her the secrets of her body. Coaxed her into the most amazing orgasm that she could still feel trembling underneath her skin.

He had said the first time could be emotional and she had laughed it off. But her emotions were shaken. Tumbled about. Confused by the storm of passion that had powered through her. Her body felt different. Her senses were turned to a different radar frequency. The glow of satiation fanned out over every inch of her flesh, each muscle and sinew softened in lassitude.

Daisy ran her hands up and down his spine, stroking and caressing the strongly muscled flesh, wondering if he had experienced anything out of the ordinary or if this was another day at the office, so to speak. She knew it would be foolish indeed to put too much significance on their lovemaking. Chemistry was chemistry. Some people connected well physically. It didn't mean they were necessarily ideal partners, for so many other factors came into play in order to sustain a long-term relationship. That she had connected so well with Luiz might just be her inexperience clouding her judgement. He had so many partners to compare her to. He was probably measuring her by them even now.

After a long moment he lifted his head to look down at her. 'I know what you're thinking.'

Daisy traced the stubble that surrounded his mouth with one of her fingertips. 'So tell me.'

His gaze went back and forth between each of her eyes. His eyes were so dark they looked like pools of black ink. 'You want to know if it was different for me.'

She made herself hold his gaze but hoped she gave little away in her own. 'Was it?'

He pushed back her hair from her face with a hand that was so gentle it felt like a feather. 'It was.'

'Because I was a virgin.'

'Not just that.'

'Then what?'

He sent his fingertip down the slope of her nose. 'I've never made love to a woman like you.'

'Fat, do you mean?'

He frowned. 'Why are you so hard on yourself? You're beautiful.'

Daisy wanted to believe him but years of self-doubt were not going to be erased that easily. She might have pranced around in that tiny bikini as if she didn't have a care in the world but she had been sucking in her tummy the whole time. 'I'm probably taking up twice the space in your bed as your other partners.'

His expression darkened as he moved away to deal with the condom. 'That's ridiculous.'

She rolled over to her stomach to watch as he went in search of his clothes. 'You're angry.'

He pulled on his jeans and zipped them up roughly. 'No, I'm not.'

'Then why are you frowning so heavily?'

He blew out a frustrated-sounding breath. 'So I date models. Is that a crime?'

Daisy propped her chin on her folded over hands, seesawing her bent legs behind her. There seemed no point hiding her nakedness now. He'd seen all there was to see. Besides, lying on her tummy meant she didn't have to concentrate on holding it in. 'Why do you date them?'

He gave her a worldly look. 'Why do you think?'

She rolled her lips together as she studied him thoughtfully. 'I don't think it's about their looks. It's their lifestyle. They're on the move like you. Another city. Another hotel. Another catwalk. They're free agents like you. That's the appeal. They won't make any demands on you.'

He gave a laugh as he reached for his shirt, thrusting his arms through and loosely buttoning it. 'I must've been mad to approach you in the bar last night.'

Daisy widened her eyes. 'Was it only last night? Gosh, I feel like I've known you for ever.'

He snatched up his phone. 'I have a couple of calls to make. Excuse me.'

'That's another thing I've noticed about you.'

He turned from the door leading into the lounge area, his expression tight with tension. 'I don't suppose you'll refrain from telling me even if I expressly ask you not to?'

She smiled sweetly. 'See? You know me so well too.'

He leaned one shoulder on the door jamb in an indolent fashion. 'Go on. Tell me what you've noticed.'

Daisy looked at the pulse that was beating at the side of his mouth. 'Intimacy scares you. And no, I'm not talking about sex. That requires very little intimacy. It's just bodies rubbing up against each other. Anyone can do that.'

His top lip curled. 'Or a machine.'

'Excellent point.'

The cynical gleam was back in his eyes. 'One would hope you enjoyed the man more than the machine?'

Daisy rolled over onto her back and tilted her head over the edge of the bed to look at him upside down. 'Are you fishing for compliments, Luiz Valquez?'

His eyes feasted on her hungrily. She had never felt such feminine power before. It made her forget her doubts about her body. He made no secret of the fact her body delighted him. The way he looked at her heated her flesh in anticipation of his touch. He wanted her even though he was trying to distance himself. It was what he did when he felt cornered. He didn't want to want her more than once. She saw the battle play out over his face as his gaze ran over her naked breasts and beyond. Stay or go. Stay or go.

'You want to play some more, *querida?*'

She gave him a vampish smile. 'Edward can go as long as I want him to.'

'Did you bring him with you?'

She sent him an arch look. 'What do you think?'

He came back over to her and traced a lazy pathway from her sternum to her mound, stopping just above the seam of her body. 'You are the most bewitching woman I've ever met.'

Daisy basked in the compliment like a fur seal in the sun. His finger was tantalisingly close to where she most wanted him. The ache was building deep inside her, all of her nerves dancing in anticipation of that first delicious stroke of his finger. His eyes grew darker and darker with desire as they held hers. Then, ever so slowly, he separated her folds, slipping one finger into the silky wetness of her body. She arched her spine like a cat, all but purring as he began to stroke her. It was impossible not to come. She didn't even have to concentrate or empty her mind of distracting thoughts. The sensations triggered by his magical touch were so intense they took over her body as if she were a rag doll, shaking her senseless.

But he didn't stop there.

He unzipped his jeans, stepping out of them roughly before reaching for another condom. She watched as he peeled it back over his length, proud and strong and virile.

He came over her, nudging her legs further apart, his eyes black and glittering as his hands pinned her arms above her head in a masterful manner, making everything that was female in her shudder in primal pleasure. She gasped as he sheathed himself to the hilt, the sensation of him stretching her to capacity sending her senses reeling. There was no slow and considerate pacing this time. He set a ruthlessly fast rhythm that made her nerves come vibrantly alive. Her body welcomed the sensual assault, delighting in the way he was thrusting with such relentless vigour as if the desire he felt for her was an unstoppable force. His face was clenched tight as he fought for control, his breathing rough and hectic.

She cried out loud as the first wave of her release hit her. It ricocheted through her body, shaking her, rattling her, sending her spinning off into a vortex that was beyond the reach of all thought and reason.

But she was still conscious enough to be aware of him as he spilled. He gave one deep sound that sounded as primitive as a feral growl, his face contorting with pleasure as he emptied.

Daisy released a shuddering breath as he released his grip on her arms. 'You really know how to give a girl a good time.' She rubbed at her tingling arms, wondering if she would bruise.

He frowned as his gaze went to the reddened marks on her skin. 'Did I hurt you?'

She suddenly felt embarrassed. She didn't want to come across as fragile. She wanted to be his equal, not some vapid wimp who didn't know how to play the casual dating game. 'Not at all.'

He ran his fingers over the marks in a barely-there touch. 'I'm sorry. I lost my head there for a bit.'

Daisy tiptoed her fingers up and down his chest. 'You don't like losing control, do you?'

'It's not a habit of mine.'

She circled each of his nipples in turn. 'There are some things in life you can't control.'

'Young, smart-mouthed Englishwomen being one of them.'

She smiled at him. 'The more I get to know you, the better I like you.'

Something flashed over his face. A camera shutter quick movement that left a nerve ticking in his jaw. 'Let's stick to the rules, shall we?'

'Oh, I'm not changing the goalposts,' she reassured him. 'Why would I? You're not what I'm looking for in a husband.'

'So you keep reminding me.'

'Why does that annoy you?'

His frown brought his brows together. 'It doesn't annoy me.'

Daisy reached up and smoothed out the crease between his eyes. 'Yes, it does.'

He pushed her hand away and got off the bed. 'I have to—'

'I know, I know,' she said with a knowing smile. 'You have to make some calls or check some emails, right?'

He shifted his lips from side to side as if wondering what to do with her. 'What is it you want from me?'

'I told you. A holiday fling. Sex without strings.'

He raked a hand through his hair, releasing a harsh-sounding breath. 'You expect me to believe that?'

'Why not?'

He stepped back into his jeans and pulled up the zip. 'Because it doesn't usually work that way.'

'You mean because women usually want the fairy-tale ending?'

'Don't you?'

'Yes, but not with you.'

He looked about to ask something but changed his mind. His mouth slammed shut as he glowered at her. But, for all that, the unspoken words rang in the silence: *Why not me?*

Daisy decided to answer anyway and ticked off her fingers as if checking off a list. 'One. You're a player, not a stayer. Two. You live in Argentina and I live in England. Three. You're—'

'Spare me the rest,' he muttered. 'I think I get the picture.'

She swung her legs off the bed and reached for the bathrobe, making a little moue with her mouth. 'I thought men were supposed to be all soft and mellow after sex? You're a big old grouch.'

He let out a just audible curse. 'I'm going to have a shower.'

'Is that code for "you're pressing my buttons"?' she asked innocently.

He caught her by the ties of the bathrobe and pulled her roughly to him. 'No,' he said. 'It's code for "I haven't finished pressing yours".'

Luiz left Daisy sleeping while he read through the sponsorship contract that had come through on email. But his gaze kept tracking back to the bed, where she lay with her cheek resting on one of her hands. Her hair was spread out over his pillow, her kiss-swollen mouth slightly parted. His groin tingled at the memory of her mouth beneath his, the way her tongue played and flirted with his.

He glanced at the bedside clock. Midnight. The second night he'd spent with her. The first one he'd spent watching her sleep. The second one he'd spent making love with her and wondering how he was going to let her go at the end of their affair.

Was this how his brother felt watching Teddy sleep? This inexplicable feeling of tenderness he couldn't shake off, no matter how much he wanted to?

Daisy didn't belong in his life. He had no time for a relationship. He wasn't relationship material—a fact she kept reminding him of at annoyingly regular intervals. He was the first to list his inadequacies. He didn't need her to spell them out for him. He knew he was unreliable in a relationship. He got bored easily. He liked to get out first before someone left him.

But for the first time in a long time—possibly ever—he didn't want to leave. He wanted to see Daisy wake up in the morning, blink those big baby-blues at him a couple of times and then smile that radiant smile that made something in his chest squeeze tight. He wanted to sit opposite her and watch her eat her breakfast like a child who had been let loose in a candy store. He wanted to see her embrace her sensuality even more, to indulge her senses without the hang-ups she had about her body. How she could doubt her physical beauty astonished him. She might not be as reed-thin as some of the models he'd dated but she had an inner beauty that was even more alluring.

He liked her sense of playfulness. She could be serious when she needed to be but a smile was never far away. He liked the way her smile lit up her eyes so they danced and sparkled.

She burrowed further into the pillow, her eyelids flickering, just like they'd done the first night he had watched her sleep. Her skin was free of make-up, as pure and as smooth as milk. He could spend hours watching her. The peacefulness of her when she slept calmed him. It soothed that restless energy deep inside him.

He came over to the bed and touched her creamy cheek with his fingertip, tracing the aristocratic slope, watching as her eyelids flickered again before opening to meet his gaze. 'What time is it?' she asked.

'Just gone midnight.'

She sat up and pushed her hair back over one shoulder, holding the sheet up to her chest to cover her nakedness. 'Have I missed dinner?'

He couldn't hold back a smile as he traced her cheekbone again. 'Do you think of anything but food?'

Her cheek bloomed pink under the brushstroke of his fingertip. 'I do now.'

Luiz bent down to press his mouth against the lush bow of hers. It never failed to amaze him how soft her lips were. Soft and pliable as they moved against his in a kiss that spoke of physical yearnings that simmered under the surface. He cupped her face and deepened the kiss, putting his knee on the bed beside her as he pressed her back down on the bed. Her arms went around his neck, her mouth hot and tempting beneath his. He explored every corner of her sweetness, the taste of her like an intoxicating elixir. He wondered if he could ever satisfy his craving for her. He was trying not to overwhelm her with too much too soon. Her body would be tender and sore if he made love to her too vigorously and too often. It was strange territory for him to be feeling so protective.

It was strange for him to be *feeling…*

He pulled back as she reached for him. 'You need food.'

'I need you more.'

He stood and put some distance between himself and her tempting body. 'Food first.'

While he was on the phone ordering room service he watched her slip on a bathrobe. She gave a little wincing movement as she walked away from the bed. Something slipped in his stomach. He'd hurt her. 'Are you OK?'

She gave him one of her bright smiles. 'Of course.'

He put the phone down and came over to her, tipping up her chin to look deep into her clear blue gaze. 'I was too rough with you.'

Her forehead pleated in a protesting frown. 'No, you weren't.'

He stroked her reddened chin where his stubble had prickled her soft skin. He heard her breath softly catch. Saw her pupils dilate. Watched as the tip of her tongue came out to dart over her lips. Felt his own body quake with want as she put her hands on his chest. Her pelvis was within a millimetre of his. He could feel the magnetic pull of her body drawing him inexorably towards her. His erection swelled, tightened, ached. It was all he could do not to crush her to him and slake the wild lust that threatened to overwhelm him.

He put his hands over hers and gently but firmly removed them from his chest. 'You need to pace yourself, *querida*. We have plenty of time.'

'Three days…or is it two now that today's over?'

Luiz ignored the odd little ache below his heart as he selected a bottle of champagne from the minibar. He popped the cork and poured two glasses, handing one to her. 'It's two.'

She took a sip of the champagne, wrinkling up her nose like a bunny as the bubbles fizzed. 'I really shouldn't be drinking this. Before you know it, I'll be spilling all my secrets.'

'Feel free.'

She laughed and set her glass down. 'Not unless you tell me one of yours first.'

Luiz leaned against the arm of the sofa. 'I don't have any. The press take care of that.'

He was acutely conscious of her gaze as it rested on him as if she were peeling back the mask of indifference he wore. He had spent most of his life pretending not to care what people said or thought about him. He had especially perfected the art in the company of his mother. He never let his mother think she had the power to hurt him. While Alejandro silently brooded over their mother's critical comments, Luiz actively encouraged them, laughing them off as if life was one big game. He enjoyed the lovable bad boy role. He'd been doing it for so long it felt normal…and yet, when Daisy looked at him with that thoughtful gaze, he wondered if she could see a tiny glimpse of the sensitive boy he had once been.

'All right,' Daisy said. 'I'll go first. I once ate a whole block of milk chocolate and burned the wrapper in the fireplace so my father wouldn't find out.'

'How old were you?'

She gave him a sheepish look. 'Twenty-three.'

'Are you joking?'

'Sadly, no.'

Luiz frowned. 'What is his problem?'

'Control is his problem. He finds it hard to love someone without controlling them. It drove my mother nuts.'

'Why do you put up with it?'

She dropped her shoulders on an expelled breath. 'I think deep down he means well. Besides, he's the only family I've got.'

'Yes, but this is the only life you've got. You can't live it according to his standards.'

'I know. That's why I came to Vegas with the girls. He didn't want me to go but for once I put my foot down.'

'Clearly not hard enough if he sent a bodyguard.'

'Yes, well, that's my dad for you.'

There was a knock on the door, announcing the arrival of the midnight supper Luiz had ordered. He tipped the young staff member and closed the door.

Daisy was staring at the tray of food as if she hadn't seen a meal for a year. 'Is this all for us?' she asked.

'It's just a snack.'

She touched a tentative hand to the tiered plate of ribbon sandwiches and buttery savoury scones. 'I swear I'm going to chain myself to the treadmill when I get home.'

Luiz watched as she picked up a salmon and asparagus sandwich, biting into it with her small white teeth, her eyes closing in bliss. There was something so sexy about the way she ate. She savoured every mouthful, licking her lips and groaning in pleasure.

She caught him watching her and blushed again. 'That's the problem with denying yourself something. Whatever's taboo is the thing you end up wanting the most.'

Isn't that the truth? Luiz thought. He hoped his expression was giving nothing away of the struggle he was enduring to keep his hands to himself. He wanted her so badly it was a throbbing ache. Worse than hunger. Worse than thirst. It was like being addicted to a potent drug. The craving ate away at his self-control until he could think of nothing but sinking into her hot, warm tightness. 'Isn't that what holidays are for? Relaxing the rules a bit?'

'Maybe.' She picked up a wedge of Camembert

cheese and looked at it balefully. 'There's more fat in this piece of cheese than in that whole plate of sandwiches.' She gave a deep sign and put the cheese back down. 'No. I'd better be good.'

Luiz picked up the cheese and held it in front of her mouth. 'Be bad. Be very bad.'

Her eyes twinkled as she opened her mouth for him to pop the cheese in. 'Mmm. That is *soooo* good.'

He wiped a tiny crumb from the corner of her mouth with the pad of his thumb, trying his best not to think of her mouth feasting on him. His attempt to keep a lid on his desire for her was taking a battering. Everything about her turned him on. The way she spoke in that husky tone. The way her eyes kept slipping to his mouth as if she couldn't help herself. The way she stood so close to him he could feel the warmth of her body and could smell the fragrance of her perfume like a sensual mist teasing his nostrils.

He gave himself a mental shake and reached for the champagne bottle. 'Top up?'

She put her hand over the top of her glass. 'And have me spilling all my secrets without you telling me one of yours? Play fair. How about you tell me something you haven't told anyone else before?'

Luiz pushed his lips from side to side, weighing up whether to take up her challenge. Hadn't he already told her more than he'd told anyone else? But something about her cute dimples and pretty blue eyes made him give in. 'OK.' He took a deep breath and slowly released it. 'I hate spiders.'

Her eyes rounded. 'Really? Like totally freaked out, stand screaming on a chair hate them?'

He gave her a look. 'No. I can actually manage to remove them without any outbursts of hysteria.'

She screwed up her nose. 'You mean like...pick them up?'

Luiz suppressed the urge to brush the skin of his arms. Talking about spiders always made him feel as if a dozen of them were tiptoeing over his flesh. 'Not with my bare hands. That's what a vacuum cleaner is for.'

'But you're six foot four tall. What's a teensy weensy little spider going to do to you?'

'Some of them are poisonous.'

She perched on the arm of the sofa, her mouth wreathed in a teasing smile. 'Don't worry. If a big, bad old spider comes sneaking in I'll save you from it.'

He drained his glass and set it back down. 'Thanks. Appreciate it.'

'I suppose you don't run across them all that often in penthouse suites.'

'You'd be surprised.'

She twirled her glass for a moment. 'I guess you must have felt so frightened and anchorless when your mum left.'

Luiz shrugged. 'I got over it.'

'I was devastated when my mum was killed.' She put her glass down and looked at him again. 'I didn't believe it at first. I thought my dad was lying. I thought she'd left him as she'd threatened to do a couple of times.' Her gaze fell away from his. 'But then I saw the police arrive...'

Luiz put a hand on her shoulder and gave it a gentle squeeze. 'I'm sorry.'

She looked up at him again. 'Do you know what was really awful?'

'What?'

'My father refused to allow me to go to the funeral. I begged and pleaded but he wouldn't listen.' Her frown was so heavy it made her look fierce in a cute and endearing way. 'He said a funeral was no place for a child. So I held my own for her. I got all my dolls and toys and took them down to the rose garden. I even made a special shrine for her out of modelling clay. I had to make the gardener, Robert, promise not to tell my father. We hid it behind her favourite rose bush. It's still there.'

'You must have loved her very much.'

She smiled a sad-looking smile. 'Yes, but don't all children love their mothers?'

Luiz thought of the shallowness of his mother. Of the way she cut down his brother every chance she got. Of the way she had insulted Teddy at the cocktail party Luiz had held recently, seeming to enjoy the hurt and cruelty she inflicted. How she publicly fawned over him as if he could do no wrong, treating him like a favourite toy instead of a son she would give her life for. 'Not all.'

Daisy put her hand over his on her shoulder. 'You hate your mother?'

Luiz gave her a rueful look. 'So, Miss Daisy, you've uncovered another well-kept secret.'

She brought his hand down to her lap, stroking the back of it with her soft fingers. 'Maybe she can't help being the way she is. Some people are not good at being parents. I see it all too often. They have this idea of how their child will be but the child is someone else entirely. They're not blank slates when they're born. They're their own little person. You can't make them into something they're not.'

Luiz suddenly had a vision of Daisy with a brood of kids around her. Not just the ones she taught, but her own children. He could imagine a little girl with a dimpled smile and bright eyes and chestnut hair and creamy skin. He thought of a little boy with—

He jerked back from where his thoughts were heading. Kids meant commitment. Long-term commitment. A lifetime of commitment and care and concern and responsibility.

But, even so, an image kept popping into his head of a little boy with black hair and brown eyes, with a little starfish hand reaching for his…

'You shouldn't hate her, Luiz.' Daisy's soft voice jolted him out of his daydream. 'Hate is such a destructive emotion.'

Luiz took a tendril of her hair and curled it around his finger. 'I should let you get back to bed.'

'Aren't you coming too?'

He tucked the hair behind her ear. 'You need a rest.'

'But I'm not tired.'

'I saw you wince when you got off the bed.'

She suddenly scowled at him and pushed his hand away to fold her arms across her body. 'I wish you wouldn't treat me like I'm made of glass. It reminds me too much of my father. Telling me what's good for me as if I couldn't possibly know myself.'

Luiz drew in a long breath through his nostrils. 'I'm sorry for being so considerate. Maybe I should just throw you down on the bed and take my pleasure without any thought of yours, like that creep you picked up the other night would've done if I hadn't stepped in.'

Her scowl fell away and her teeth bit down on her lower lip. 'I'm sorry.'

'Forget about it.'

She came over to him and put a hand on his arm, looking up at him with those beautiful lake-blue eyes. 'You let everyone think you're a caddish man-about-town but you're the most gentle and considerate man I've ever met.'

He put his hands on her upper arms, tensing his fingers just enough to remind her of the strength he had at his disposal. He felt her shiver under his touch and his body responded with a rocket blast of lust. He brought his mouth down to hers, shocked at the heat that exploded as his lips came into contact with hers. Her tongue tangled with his in a sexy duel that made his whole body vibrate with longing. Blood surged hot and strong to his groin, swelling him against the urgent press of her body.

He slipped her robe off her shoulders, letting it fall to the floor at her feet. His hands moved over her silky flesh, cupping and shaping her until she whimpered her delight into his mouth. He moved his hands down over her hips, holding her to the throb of his need. She moved against him, wriggling her body to get closer.

He picked her up and carried her back to the bedroom, sliding her down the length of his body as he lowered her feet to the floor. Her mouth stayed locked on his, her tongue playing with his in an erotic dance that fired his blood. Her hands were everywhere—in his hair, moving up and down his back and shoulders, cupping his buttocks, touching him and stroking him until he was so primed he had to fight for control.

He bent her back down on the bed, rolling her over so she straddled him. Her hair cascaded over her shoulders, half covering her breasts in a sexy pose that thrilled his senses. He reached for a condom from the bedside drawer and sheathed himself. 'This way you can control the depth,' he said.

She placed her hands either side of his head and lowered herself onto him, her mouth opening on a soft little gasp as her body accepted him. He kept his movements to a minimum, letting her do the work so she could control how much of him she took in. She began to move, slowly rocking, then building the pace as she found her sweet spot.

He began to move with her, taking her with him on a wave of pleasure that travelled through his body until he could hold back no longer. He felt her contract around him in tight spasms of release that triggered his own. He lost all thought as he gave himself to the moment of exhilaration, that wonderful moment when his body broke free from all restraints and soared.

He held her to his chest as she collapsed over him, her hair tickling his face and chest. He stroked his hand in lazy circles up and down her spine, over the curve of her bottom and then back up again. Breathing in the scent of her skin, the summer flowers and sensual woman fragrance that thrilled his senses in a way no other woman had before.

'Your hands are like exfoliation gloves,' she said against his ear.

Luiz felt a smile tug on his lips. 'Glad I'm proving to be so useful.'

She raised herself up to look at him with a playful expression. 'Are we done?'

'Not yet.'

Her eyes danced in anticipation. 'You mean you can go another round?'

Luiz rolled her off him and got off the bed and held out his hand to her. 'Come on.'

'Where are we going?'

'I scrubbed your back. Now it's time for you to scrub mine.'

Before she knew it, Daisy was in the shower recess with him, naked and slippery with bath gel. Her mouth was locked beneath his in a searing kiss, his hands moving over her body in caressing waves that made her skin tingle all over. The combination of the stinging needles of water as well as his calloused hands was enough to send her senses haywire. He came to her breasts and subjected them to a torturous massage, stopping only to suckle on each of her nipples before resuming his mind-blowing stroking. He moved down her body, dipping his fingers between her thighs, tantalising her with little touches and fleeting strokes that stirred her desire to fever-pitch. She shamelessly rubbed herself against his hand, whimpering as the water coursed over her face and shoulders.

He slipped a finger inside her but it wasn't enough. She wanted him. All of him.

She reached for him, holding him in her hand, stroking the velvet-covered hardness until he had to brace himself against the shower stall. Emboldened by his response to her touch, she slipped to her knees and traced her tongue over him from base to tip. He shuddered and smothered a groan and she became bolder, using her whole mouth this time to draw on him. She felt his blood thundering as she moved her mouth up and down, varying the speed and suction, testing what he liked, going purely on instinct and being rewarded by his passionate response.

'Enough,' he groaned and pulled away, breathing heavily as he hauled her upright.

Daisy looked into his lust-glazed eyes and a frisson of excitement washed over her. 'I wanted to make you come.'

'I don't think there's any danger of that not happening.' He took a handful of her wet hair, bringing her head closer to kiss her deeply.

She moved against his hard body, wriggling so his erection was against her folds. She reached for him again and guided him towards her.

He suddenly stalled. 'Are you on the Pill?'

'Yes.'

He seemed to be hesitating, his body poised at her entrance. 'I don't usually do this.'

'It's not as if I've been with anyone else, so if that's what's—'

'It's not that.' He brushed the wet hair back from her

forehead, his gaze trained on hers. 'It's a boundary I've never crossed before.'

Daisy placed her hand on his chest where his heart was thumping. 'So it will be your first time too. That kind of makes us even, doesn't it?'

His mouth kicked up at one corner. 'There's something really screwy about your logic but I'm going to go with it for once.'

She smiled back and moved closer, enticing him with her body, rolling her hips and brushing her breasts against his chest, watching in delight as his eyes darkened even further.

He hooked one of her legs over his hip as he drove into her with a strong thrust that made the breath whoosh out of her lungs. Pleasure shot through her as her body surrounded him tightly. He began to move within her, each thrust delivering more friction against her sensitised nerves. The water poured down over their bodies in a warm flow that added to the eroticism of the moment.

His hands cupped the cheeks of her bottom firmly as he increased the pace, holding her in a sensual lock that she caught sight of in the mirror out of the corner of her eye. The image of their bodies locked in passion was so arousing she felt every erogenous zone on her body quake in reaction.

He caught her eye in the mirror and gave her a bad boy smile that made her inner core clench. He turned her so she was facing the mirror full on with him behind her. He entered her again, this most alpha and primitive of positions making her legs tremble as she saw the glinting delight in his gaze. Feeling his powerful thrusts from behind heightened her pleasure in a way she hadn't thought possible. The slight tilt of her hips, the sexy rocking in his body, the sheer wildness and wickedness of doing it in front of a mirror made her senses sing with rapture. The orgasm came upon her like a thrashing wave, rushing through her like a bullet train, spitting her out the other side until she felt limbless.

But Luiz was still holding her upright, his strong thighs braced either side of hers as he prepared to let himself fly free. Daisy watched him as he pumped his way to a cataclysmic release. All of his facial muscles tensed, his breathing deep and heavy as he gave a series of surging thrusts that tipped him over the edge. He gave a wild groan as he emptied himself, his hands still fastened like manacles on her hips. She felt the warm spill of his essence between her thighs, such a raw and intimate coupling with her own moisture.

He turned her to face him and took her mouth in a long deep kiss as the water cascaded over their faces and their bodies.

Daisy stroked her hands over his warm wet chest, angling her head so he could take his kiss down the slope of her neck. The scrape of his stubble on her skin made her shiver in delight. Was there no end to the magic this man could do to her? She had gone from being a sexually shy, body issue plagued virgin to a steamy, flirty wanton in less than forty-eight hours.

But in four weeks' time her exotic fling would be over and so too would her walk on the wild side. Facing the long, cold bleakness of winter would be even worse now she had experienced such scorching heat. Would her new confidence disappear under layers of winter woollies or would the part of her Luiz had brought out stay out?

Luiz threaded his hands through the wet curtain of her hair, holding her head steady as he meshed his gaze with hers. 'So, we're even.'

Daisy pressed her belly against his iron-hard abdomen. Oh, for muscles as toned as that, she thought. 'You've never done it uncovered before?'

'No.'

She outlined his mouth with her fingertip. 'That's very responsible of you.'

A shadow passed through his gaze. 'How long have you been on the Pill?'

She gave him a self-deprecating look. 'Five years. How's that for wishful thinking?'

His deep frown gave him an intimidating air. 'I can't believe what's wrong with your countrymen. If it'd been up to me I would've sorted you out at the age of consent.'

She sent him a provocative smile. 'Sort me out? What on earth does that mean?'

He reached for her again and brought his mouth down to hers. 'I'll show you.'

CHAPTER NINE

'SO HOW'S THE hot fling going?' Belinda asked Daisy when they met up briefly for a quick shop on day three of the holiday.

'Too fast.' Daisy allowed herself the smallest of shoulder slumps at the thought of flying home in the morning.

The last three days had gone past in a whirlwind of late breakfasts and long, lazy lunches and dinners and spectacular shows and late suppers. Dancing in night-clubs until the wee hours, a drive out to the desert in an Italian sports car with a gourmet picnic and a rug to indulge in a champagne supper under the stars. Passionate nights in Luiz's arms, making love in every room, in every position and even inventing some of their own.

How was her quiet ordinary life in London ever going to compare?

'But you're seeing him back in London, right?' Kate said.

'That's the plan...'

'If you ask me, I think you're crazy to continue with him,' Belinda said. 'A holiday fling is meant to be just that. Once the holiday is over, that's it. *Finito.* You're not supposed to see each other again.'

'But what if they're in love?' Kate said.

Belinda gave Daisy a beady look. 'Are you?'

Daisy laughed it off. 'Of course not.'

'Sure?'

No. 'Yes.'

Falling in love with someone like Luiz Valquez would prove once and for all how ridiculously naïve she was. Thinking for a moment someone like him would be interested in spending the rest of his life with her was about as deluded as anyone could get. He was ready to move on. Sure, he'd been charming and sweet and caring but she'd seen him watching her with a frown one too many times. He was probably planning to ditch her before she left for London. Why wouldn't he? He wouldn't want the inconvenience of a long distance relationship, even if it were only for another four weeks. He would want to get back to his fly-in, fly-out lifestyle.

'What about Luiz?' Kate asked.

'What about him?' Daisy said.

'What does he feel about you?'

'Lust,' Belinda said with an eye roll. 'Didn't you see that video clip on Twitter someone posted last night? I didn't know you could do the tango, Daze. It looked like you were having sex with him on that dance floor.'

Daisy could feel a blush stealing over her entire body at the thought of how she and Luiz had burned up the dance floor late last night. He had turned it into a form of foreplay. Her whole body had been vibrating with lust by the time they got back to his suite. Their need for each other had been so explosive they hadn't even bothered removing their clothes but shoved them out of the way instead. 'He's an excellent teacher.'

'Not just on the dance floor, one presumes,' Belinda said. 'You've got that look.'

She was almost afraid to ask. 'What look is that?'

'The I've-just-had-the-best-sex-of-my-life look.'

'All I can say is good on you, Daisy.' Kate leaned forward to refill her wine glass. 'It's not like we've been so lucky, have we, Belinda?'

'Just because neither of us has been wined and dined and seduced out of our senses by a hot Argentinian playboy doesn't mean we haven't had a good time,' Belinda said with a little scowl.

'But what about those guys you were dancing with the other night?' Daisy asked.

Belinda gave a snort. 'Turns out they were married.'

'Oh…'

Kate raised her glass in a toast. 'To Daisy's first fling.'

Belinda clinked her glass against Daisy's. 'Let's hope you end it before it's too late.'

Luiz took a sip of his drink as he waited for Daisy to join him in the bar. She had spent a couple of hours that afternoon with her girlfriends shopping, claiming she couldn't possibly go back home without a quick trip to the outlet mall. After appearing in that skimpy fuchsia-pink bikini the other day, he was starting to wonder what she might come back with. As much as it thrilled him to see her in such a racy little number, or indeed nothing at all, he had other concerns right now. After the smoking-hot clip someone had loaded on social media of them doing the tango last night, he was expecting someone to sneak up behind him with a baseball bat. If word got back to Charles Wyndham that Luiz was corrupting his baby girl with raunchy dancing and porn star bikinis and God knew what else, he would be limping around on crutches for sure.

What had happened to his determination to keep his hands off her? What a joke. He hadn't lasted twenty-four hours. The last three days had been some of the most sensually pleasing of his life. *The* most sensually pleasing. Who was he kidding? No one came close to rocking his world the way Daisy did.

A vision of them in the shower together flashed through his brain. His body hardened at the memory. His skin shivered beneath his clothes, his desire for her ramping up until it was all he could think about. Her gorgeous and totally natural body, her breasts and womanly hips, the soft feminine swell of her belly that was such a contrast to the toned strength of his. The way she had stroked and worshipped his body with such honesty, responding to him with her whole being, her shyness melting away as she discovered the intimate secrets of her womanhood. He had seen it all played out on her face—the wonder, the joy, the rapture. He felt a part of it in a way he had never felt with another partner. She gave herself to him in a way no one had ever done before. And not just because she was a virgin, although he'd be lying if he didn't admit that had triggered some Neanderthal-like pleasure deep in his psyche.

Daisy was an old-fashioned girl with a wicked and playful side he found enormously attractive. The only thing he found a little irritating was her candour. She had a tendency to speak her mind, most particularly her observations about him. He'd made the fatal error of revealing too much to her over that first breakfast. Somehow, watching her gobble up that meal like a kid in a candy store had made him lower his guard. She might have the appearance of being a little naïve but underneath that guileless dimpled smile was a smart young woman who knew much more than she let on.

But was she being straight with him about what she wanted out of their relationship? She claimed she only wanted him for sex. It was the same claim he had made to all the women he'd slept with over the years. Why then did it niggle him so much she didn't want more? This was their last night together. She hadn't said a word about wanting more from him. Most women would have dropped a hint or two by now. But she had said nothing. Zilch. He wasn't even sure if she was going to agree to see him in London. What if she changed her mind? What if she decided what happened in Vegas had to stay in Vegas?

Not that he was thinking of settling down any time soon. He supposed there might come a day in the distant future when he would get around to thinking about acquiring a suitable wife, maybe having a couple of kids to keep his branch of the family tree going. But it wasn't on his radar at the moment. Besides, Alejandro and Teddy would see to all that traditional stuff, which would leave him with a little more breathing room.

In the past, whenever he'd thought of settling down he'd got a claustrophobic feeling. A cold dread would fill him. He would feel suffocated by the thought of being tied down to one woman.

But that was before he'd met Daisy with her sparkling smile and winsome ways.

As soon as he'd laid eyes on her he had felt something thump him in the chest. Her clear blue eyes had met his across the crowded room and her uppity little nose had inched ever so higher. The rush of his blood had almost knocked him off his feet. Lust had rocketed through him as soon as he saw the defiant way she looked at him. The denial of her attraction to him had been a potent turn-on. The fact she hadn't known who he was had been a bonus. He was growing weary of the groupies who trailed after him and his mates for the sake of bedding a professional sportsman. They weren't interested in him as a person. They didn't know a brass razoo about him. They knew nothing about who he was beneath the brash, fun-loving mask.

There were times when he didn't know himself...

Luiz drowned the thought with another sip of his drink but, as he lowered his glass, he saw Daisy enter the bar. It was like a bizarre rerun of the first night they had met. He felt the same knockout punch to his chest as her eyes met his across the floor. But this time she didn't put her nose in the air. Instead, she gave him a smouldering come-and-get-me look that made the back of his neck fizz and prickle in excitement.

His eyes nearly popped out of his head and landed in his drink when he ran his gaze over her outfit. So too did every other man's. Gone was the conservative little black dress.

Her dress was a tight-fitting leather sheath that clung to her body like a sleek evening glove. The neckline plunged between her breasts, giving cheeky little glimpses of the gentle curves of her breasts. The hemline was mid-thigh but it looked even shorter because she was wearing hooker-high heels.

Also gone was the prim and conservative schoolteacher make-up. In its place was smoky eye shadow, scarlet lipstick, bronze blush and thick black mascara and eyeliner that gave her a free love, Sixties look to match her teased, high ponytail. She was wearing dangling earrings and carrying a tiny silver evening purse and her arms were bare apart from a metallic bracelet that jangled as she sashayed towards him.

She sent a fingertip over the back of his hand in a teasing brushstroke and batted her eyelashes at him. 'Want to buy me a drink?'

'Sure.' He liked this game. If this was her idea of dress-ups he was in. 'What will you have?'

'Champagne.'

'French?'

She gave him a worldly look. 'Is there any other?'

Luiz had never felt more turned on by a woman. She was vampish and yet underneath all the war paint and costuming he could see the essence of purity and wholesomeness that made her so unique. He ordered the champagne and when it arrived he ushered her to a more private area where velvet sofas were stationed in a cosy nook.

She sat down opposite him and elegantly crossed one leg over the other, her dazzling smile brighter than the surrounding lighting.

He handed her a bubbling glass of champagne. 'I see the shopping trip was successful.'

'Very.' She took a sip and wrinkled up her nose as the bubbles danced. That was another thing he adored about her. All those little mannerisms she didn't try to hide in order to appear sophisticated. 'How did you spend your time?'

'I had a Skype call with the sponsors.'

'It went well?'

'Extremely.' He raised his glass to hers. 'I have a meeting with them in London the week after next. The whole board want to meet me, thanks to you whitewashing my reputation.'

She clinked her glass against his. 'To reforming irascible rakes.'

He held her gaze with smouldering heat. 'To debauching good girls.'

She laughed a tinkling bell laugh. 'Belinda can't believe the change in me. She's always told me off for being so staid and conservative. Just shows what meeting the right man can do.'

The right man? He was totally wrong for her. Hadn't her father made that clear? He hooked an eyebrow upwards. 'I'm not sure your father would think that.'

Her smile slipped away as she looked at the leaping bubbles in her glass. 'For years I've always done what he said. I was happy to do it. It was easier than arguing with him. But over the last few months I started to feel like life was leaving me behind.' Her gaze came back to his. 'That's why this trip here was so important. I had to shake off the old Daisy and embrace the new. I'm not sure I would've been able to do it at home.'

'So what happens when you go back tomorrow? Will you slip back into good habits again?'

Her dimples appeared as she smiled. 'There's always that danger, I suppose.'

Luiz ran his eyes over her outfit again. 'You look hot tonight.'

She pulled at her lip with her teeth. 'You don't think it's too over the top?'

'For Vegas, no. For teaching five-year-olds in London? You may have a problem.'

A little frown flitted over her forehead as she glanced around. 'Gosh, I didn't think of that. What if someone sees me?'

'Wasn't that the whole idea?' he asked. 'To get noticed?'

'By you; not by the rest of the world.'

'It comes with the territory of hanging out with me. I attract the world's attention.'

She looked at him thoughtfully for a long moment. 'Why is being the centre of attention so important to you?'

Luiz thought of all the times as a child when his needs went unnoticed. The constant struggle to be heard in a house that had to remain quiet for the sake of his father's health. His brother had done what he could but he hadn't been able to meet the emotional needs of a young insecure child. Who would have expected him to? His mother's desertion had made Luiz act out in a variety of ways that had tested his older brother's patience. Alejandro had used work and study and doing whatever he could to keep the family together as his way of coping with the pain of their father's accident and their mother's leaving. Luiz had used any number of attention-seeking behaviours. His reputation as a tearaway began early and even though there were times when he'd wished he could reinvent himself, he'd never quite managed to do it. Although he was more than competent academically, his love and natural aptitude for sport was the thing that stood him apart from his peers. Over the years the adulation of the crowd had become more and more addictive. It made him all the more competitive and ruthlessly driven to be the best.

But it was lonely at the top and there was only one way down from it—the word he dreaded more than any other—failure.

'I'm just a ratbag,' he said lightly. 'Ask my brother. He'll tell you.'

A wistful smile curved her mouth. 'I would've loved a sister or a brother. I think my mum would've had another child but for the fact that she wasn't happy with my father.'

'Why didn't she divorce him?'

'She asked him once or twice but he always talked her out of it.' She traced her fingertip around the rim of her glass before she added, 'Arguing with my father is not for the faint-hearted. He can be very persuasive.'

Tell me about it, Luiz thought. 'What sort of husband was he to your mother?'

She looked at him with her clear blue gaze. 'Do you mean: was he abusive?'

'Is that why she wanted to leave him?'

'No, he wasn't abusive. He loved her too much, if that makes sense.' Her finger did another circuit before she looked at him again. 'He expected her to be a certain type of wife. But my mother wasn't the type of person to be boxed in.'

'Is that what he does to you? He expects you to act and behave a certain way?'

She sighed. 'Yes…I hate disappointing him. I really do. I'm all he has, when you think about it. He wants me to be happy. I totally understand that. It's what all parents want for their kids. He doesn't want me to mess up my life with being with the wrong person, I guess because of how things turned out between my mother and him. But how can I find out who's right for me if I don't put myself out there? It's not like you can just know in an instant if someone's perfect for you.'

Luiz studiously examined the contents of his half-empty glass. 'My brother said as soon as he met his wife Teddy he knew she was the one.' He met her gaze again. 'So I suppose it must happen occasionally.'

'So you believe in love at first sight?'

'I didn't say that.'

'But that's what happened with your brother.'

'Doesn't mean it will happen with me.'

She angled her head in that cute way she had. 'But it could. Statistically speaking.'

'What have statistics got to do with it?'

She shrugged and picked up her drink again. 'Your

brother sounds like a romantic. You've got a fifty per cent chance of being one as well.'

'I don't think so.'

She gave him a teasing smile. 'How do you know? You haven't met the woman of your dreams yet. But when you do—whammo—you'll be done like a turkey at Christmas.'

He gave a wry chuckle. 'The woman of my dreams doesn't exist.'

She sat back in her chair and recrossed her long legs, gently kicking one dainty ankle up and down as her gaze held his. 'Describe her to me.'

Luiz gave her a crooked smile. 'Chestnut hair, blue eyes, creamy skin, hot body and legs up to—'

She leaned forward and tapped his thigh with a playful hand. 'I'm being serious.'

So am I, he thought with a jolt. Wasn't Daisy everything he wanted? She was funny and smart. She was fun to be around. She was sweet and yet strong enough to speak her mind. She was sexy and yet she could be a perfect lady when the need arose. She had class. She was the most thrilling lover he'd ever had.

But…

He wasn't going to fall in love and have his feelings trampled over. He wasn't going to make himself vulnerable. Not to her. Not to anyone. Not again.

'What about you?' He tossed the question back. 'Describe your dream lover.'

Her gaze flicked up to the right as if she was picturing her ideal man in her mind. 'Tall, because I would hate to tower over a man when I put on a pair of heels.

Smart, because I find intelligence the biggest turn-on. Funny, because life is so serious anyway and it's important to be with someone who makes you smile. Sexy, because chemistry is so important and who wants to be with someone who doesn't make your heart go pitter-patter?'

'Anything else?'

She tapped her index finger against her lips. 'Let me see now… Ah, yes. Eyes. He has to have nice eyes.'

Luiz lifted a brow. 'What about money?'

'Not important.'

He gave a cynical laugh. 'It's always important.'

'Not to me.'

He held her gaze for a beat. 'Isn't the possession of money a sign the man has got his act together? That he has drive and ambition?'

Her clear blue gaze didn't waver. 'He might have got it through inheritance or luck, such as winning the lottery.'

'So you don't mind if he's got money as long as he's earned it himself?'

'I would overlook his affluence for other far more important qualities.'

'Such as?'

'Moral fortitude.'

Luiz laughed again. 'I guess that rules me out.'

A tiny frown tugged at her brow as she sat looking at him in silence.

'What?'

She blinked and cleared her gaze. 'Nothing.'

'Why were you frowning?'

She put her drink down and flashed him a smile. 'What does a girl have to do around here to get a guy to ask her to dance?'

Luiz led Daisy to the dance floor but, instead of the thumping music of all the nights before, there was a pianist playing a slow tempo romantic ballad. Right now she could have done with some head-banging music to knock the sprouting foolishness out of her head. What was she thinking? Luiz wasn't marriage material. He might be funny and charming and sexy and intelligent and have the nicest eyes she'd ever seen, but he was way out of her league. He was an international sports star. He was the epitome of the freedom-loving playboy. Men like Luiz Valquez did not settle down to suburbia and raise two-point-two kids. He was not the type of man to fall in love, let alone with someone like her.

No, she would be sensible and stick to the plan. She would have her fun and then it would be over. After the Grand Slam he would go back to his life and she would go back to hers. They would never meet again and she would be fine about that. She would have to be fine about it. She had no business conjuring up unrealistic scenarios. Luiz might be a lot deeper than she had first thought him but that didn't mean he would suddenly morph into ideal husband material. He would hate to be tied down to one woman. He was used to a banquet of them. She'd be lucky to even see him once during the next month. Surely he would find someone more exciting than her.

Luiz's hand rested in the small of Daisy's back. 'You've gone quiet.'

'I'm thinking.'

'About?'

She looked up at him. 'Will you see anyone else during the next month?'

His brow was deeply furrowed. 'What sort of question is that?'

'It's not like you'll be in London full-time. You might get lonely and—'

'I might seem a little loose with my morals to someone like you but I don't fool around when I'm in a relationship.'

'But we're not really in a relationship. It's just a fling.'

'Same difference.'

She looked at his frowning expression. 'I didn't mean to upset you.'

'I am *not* upset.'

She touched the corner of his mouth, where a knot of tension had gathered. 'You're grinding your teeth. I can hear it over the music. It's really bad for your molars.'

He suddenly laughed. 'I need my head read.'

Daisy peeped up at him again. 'Why? Because you're enjoying yourself and you didn't expect to?'

He brought the tip of his finger down the slope of her nose. 'I've never met anyone like you before.'

'You really need to get out more.'

He was still smiling as he pulled her close. 'Maybe I do.'

Because it was their last night together before she flew home with the girls, Luiz took Daisy to an exclusive restaurant where the chef had won numerous awards.

He had booked a private dining room for them, which added to the decadence. She drooled at the delicious food as each dish was brought to their table. A seafood starter in a delectable piquant sauce, prime fillet steak with a colourful vegetable stack and crusty bread rolls with fresh butter for mains. All artfully presented and cooked to perfection, complemented with fine wines that burst with flavour with each sip.

'My thighs are going to hate you for this,' Daisy said as she finally put down her knife and fork. 'I've eaten more in the last four days than I've eaten in the last four months. Years, even.'

He sat watching her like an indulgent uncle. 'I like to see a woman with a healthy appetite.'

'Yes, well, if only my appetite for exercise was as robust.'

His dark eyes smouldered. 'Maybe you've been doing the wrong sort of workouts.'

Daisy felt a shiver go down her spine. 'I hate exercising alone.'

'So you prefer contact sports?'

'Not until very recently.'

His mouth tipped up in a sexy smile. 'Do you want dessert and coffee or should we go and get some exercise?'

Daisy pretended to think about it. 'Hmm, let me see now...dessert or a hot, sweaty workout?'

His eyes glinted some more. 'Can I tempt you with your own personal trainer?'

She tossed her napkin on the table and pushed back her chair. 'Sold.'

* * *

Luiz pushed back the bedcovers at two a.m. and wandered over to the windows to look at the busy strip below. He hated not being able to sleep. Hour after hour of tossing and fidgeting and ruminating made his head pound. Normally he would work off his restlessness in the gym but he hadn't wanted to leave Daisy. He scoffed at his uncharacteristic sentimentality. It wasn't as if this was the end of the affair. He would be seeing her on and off in London. He was still in the driving seat. He would say when and where and for how long. The Grand Slam was supposed to be his focus, not a slip of a girl who was looking for the fairy tale. The closest he got to the fairy tale was the role of the big bad wolf. He was good at being bad. He'd spent most of his life playing up. It was his trademark.

He turned from the window to look at Daisy. She was still sleeping soundly, clearly not worried this was their last night together. She was curled up on her side, her cheek resting on one of her hands in that childlike manner she had and her hair splayed out over his pillow. The scent of her was on his sheets, on his skin, burned in his memory. He would never be able to walk past honeysuckle without thinking of her.

How had he got himself in this situation? He was feeling sick to his stomach at the thought of saying goodbye to her at the airport. He *hated* goodbyes. He loathed them with a passion. He still remembered the way his mother had swept him up in a goodbye hug and poured kisses all over his face as she left for her 'holiday'. He hadn't seen her for two years. He had spent every single day of them waiting. Hoping.

What if he never saw Daisy again? What if she changed her mind when she got back to London? Would the intimacy they'd shared be enough to keep her tied to him until the Grand Slam was over?

And then what?

He brushed the errant thought aside. His credo was 'for fun, not for ever'. He was only interested in the here and now.

Not the, then what?

CHAPTER TEN

DAISY WOKE IN the night and found the space beside her in the bed was empty. She brushed her hair out of her face and swung her legs over the side of the bed. The bedside clock showed it was almost five in the morning and while down below on the strip there was a seething mass of revellers still spilling out from hotels and clubs, the suite felt unnaturally, eerily quiet. She slipped on a bathrobe and loosely tied the waistband, and pointedly ignoring her packed suitcase in the corner, padded out to the lounge area.

Luiz was sitting in front of the large-screen television with the sound turned off. He was watching a twenty-four-hour sporting channel—she would rather watch paint dry—or at least he had been watching. Right now, he was soundly asleep.

Daisy took the opportunity to soak in his features. His dark hair was still tousled from where her fingers had threaded through it. He had slipped on a pair of boxers but the rest of his body was gloriously naked. She had run her hands over every inch of his body, worshipping him with kisses and caresses, imprinting his scent and the feel of his skin on her senses so she could revisit them when their affair was finally over.

She drifted over to the sofa, drawn to him like a magnet drew metal. Her fingers lightly touched his hair, moving through the thick dark strands as lightly as fairy feet. His breathing was deep and even, but there were shadows beneath his eyes, as if he'd taken a long time to get to sleep. His stubble was heavily shadowed along his jaw and she couldn't resist placing her fingertips on it to feel the sexy rasp of it. His eyelids flickered but his breathing remained steady.

She couldn't stop herself from touching him. He was a temptation she had no power to resist. Forget about forbidden food. *He* was her new vice.

Just as well she was leaving this morning…

She traced the outline of each of his eyebrows. She travelled her finger down the length of his nose. She leaned in close and pressed her lips to his in a kiss as soft as a moth's wing.

His eyes opened and locked on hers. 'What are you up to?'

'Watching you sleep.'

'I wasn't sleeping.'

'Yes, you were.'

His brow lifted. 'On the contrary, I was watching golf.'

Daisy gave him a wry smile. 'Well, I would be sleeping too if I had to watch that.'

His gaze went to her mouth. 'What time do you leave?'

'Eight.'

He traced her mouth with a lazy finger for a long beat of silence. 'You could stay a couple more days. I don't have to fly back to Argentina until the weekend.'

'If I didn't have a classroom of kids to worry about I might take you up on that.'

He held her gaze with an unreadable look. 'What if I cover your wages?'

Daisy pulled away to stand with her arms folded across her middle. Hurt knifed through her with shame closely on its tail. He was reducing her to *that?* Nothing more than a plaything he was prepared to *pay* for? 'You know, for a scary moment there I thought you were asking me to be your kept mistress.'

There was another beat of silence.

'Would that be a problem?'

She dropped her arms and blew out a breath. 'Of course it's a problem. I'm not one of your good time floozies. I have a career that's important to me.'

'It's only for a month.'

'A month is a long time in a child's life,' she said. 'This is the winter term. There's the Christmas pageant to organise. I have heaps to do and I can't just drop everything because you want to party a little longer.'

He rose from the sofa and shoved a hand through his hair. 'Fine. Go back to London. I'll see you when I see you.'

Daisy looked at the tight set to his back and shoulders as he faced the windows. A wall had come up and she was on the wrong side of it. 'You're asking too much, Luiz. Surely you can see that?'

He turned to look at her with an inscrutable expression. 'It was just an idea. Forget about it. Let's stick to the plan.'

'It's not that I don't want to—'

'Can I ask you to refrain from speaking to the press?' He gave her a formal smile that didn't involve his eyes. 'They have a habit of twisting things.'

Daisy turned back to the bedroom, her spirits sinking like a ship's anchor. She could feel the dragging weight of it in the pit of her stomach. How could he dismiss her so casually after the passionate night they'd spent together? Or was this the way he ended all of his hook-ups? Cleanly and coldly and clinically.

When she came back out, showered and dressed, Luiz informed her he had a taxi waiting.

She hoped she wasn't showing anything of the disappointment she was feeling. It was a tight ache in her chest like a band of steel squeezing against her heart and lungs. 'You're not coming to see me off?'

'I have a conference call with the sponsors.'

Daisy could see which way his priorities lay. She would be out of sight and out of mind. How soon before he found a replacement? Her spirits plummeted even further. How had she let this happen? Why hadn't she seen it coming? Her four days of fun had set her up for a lifetime of misery.

He handed her into the taxi and leaned down and kissed her on the mouth through the open window. 'Be safe, little English girl.' He tapped his hand on the rim of the window and then stepped back, his expression as blank as if he was seeing off an acquaintance.

Daisy waved to him as the taxi pulled away from

the hotel concourse, her heart feeling as if it was being pulled in a vicious tug-of-war. She wanted to stay but she had responsibilities she couldn't drop on a whim. But even if she had stayed, how could she agree to his terms? He wasn't offering her a future. He was offering her a position. A temporary one. A tawdry one. He wanted to grease the wheels with his sponsors. She was nothing more than a means to an end. He would achieve his goal and she would be out of his life, just like every other woman he had associated with before.

How had she been so foolish and naïve to expect anything else? Was this why her father felt she had to have someone to watch over her twenty-four seven? She couldn't be trusted to run her own life. She was too gullible. Not street smart enough to know when she was being used. Luiz Valquez wasn't the sort of man to suddenly fall in love, certainly not after only four days. How could she compete with the women who took his fancy? She was so ordinary compared to them. He would probably hook up with a replacement while she was on her way to the airport. Las Vegas was full of girls looking for a good time with a bad boy.

She had stupidly been one of them.

Belinda and Kate were waiting outside their hotel as the taxi swept in to collect them.

'Where's lover boy?' Belinda asked. 'I thought he'd be seeing you off.'

'He has more important things to do.'

Belinda gave her a probing look. 'Uh-oh.'

Daisy glowered. 'Don't start.'

'Have I taught you nothing, Daze?' Belinda's tone

was exasperated. 'How many times do I have to drum it into your thick head? You're not supposed to fall in love on a holiday fling.'

'I'm not in love with him.' If she said it enough times maybe it would be true. How could she have fallen in love with him? It was the last thing she wanted. The last thing she expected.

'Sure you're not.'

'I just think he could've had the decency to say goodbye at the airport like everyone else does.' Daisy hugged her handbag against her stomach. 'I mean, how hard is that?'

'Maybe he doesn't like saying goodbye,' Kate said.

Daisy thought about Luiz's mother leaving when he was a small child. Had she explained to him where she was going or had she just left? Had he waited for her day after day, not sure if she would ever return? She thought of him being brought up by his older brother, only a child himself, struggling to keep the family together. Their tragically injured father living out the rest of his days in sickness and dependency. Was that why Luiz was so restless and rootless? He hated being tied down. He shied away from commitment. He didn't bond with people because people always let him down one way or the other.

Wasn't that why he always had a call to make or an email to check? He used business to distance himself. It was a barrier he used to keep himself separate from anything emotional. Was he developing feelings for her—fledging feelings he didn't know how to handle? Like the feelings she wasn't even game to name? Was that why he'd put the drawbridge up, making her think his conference call was far more important than seeing her off? Was it foolish to hope she would be the one person to dismantle the defences he had built around himself?

The last four days had been much more than a sex-fest. He had taken her to dinner and shows, spent hours with her, talking about everyday matters. He had told her things he had told no one before—secrets and confidences. He had allowed her in. He seemed to enjoy her company in whatever context. All those times she'd found him looking at her with a contemplative expression on his face were surely not the product of her imagination. It was as if he was imagining the possibility of a future with her.

Or had that been just wishful thinking on her part?

As they were checking in a young man dressed in the uniform of Luiz's hotel came rushing over. 'Miss Wyndham? This is from Luiz Valquez. He asked me to give it to you.'

Daisy took the small square package. 'Thank you.'

'Aren't you going to open it?' Belinda asked.

'What is it?' Kate peered over her shoulder. 'Is it a ring?'

Daisy peeled back the giftwrap to find a small lingerie box inside, tied up with a scarlet bow. She undid the bow and opened the box and lifted out of the bed of tissue a pair of dainty lace knickers as fine as a silky cobweb. There was a card poked in amongst the tissue.

'What does it say?' Belinda jostled against her shoulder.

Daisy looked down at the dark scrawl of the letter *L*.

Belinda gave a cynical exhale. 'His initial.'

'What if it stands for love?' Kate asked.

Daisy folded her fingers over the card, her heart lifting on a faint breath of hope. 'Come on. That's our boarding call.'

It was raining when Daisy landed in London. Her father was there to meet her and ushered her out of the arrivals hall with a hand firmly at her elbow. 'You have some explaining to do, young lady,' he said. 'That clip of you dancing with Luiz Valquez has gone viral. I didn't sacrifice everything to bring you up to act like a slut the first moment I turn my back.'

'I was dancing, Dad. I was enjoying myself. You should try it some time.'

He frowned at her. 'Why him? Why not some decent guy who'd do the right thing by you? This is not what I wanted for you. You could do so much better.'

So much better than what? Daisy thought. Who could be better than Luiz? He was everything she wanted. She couldn't imagine wanting anyone else. He had awakened her with his touch. Her body responded to him as if it had been waiting for him all this time. How could she settle for anyone else with the memory of his caresses still echoing throughout her body?

'Attraction doesn't work that way,' she said. 'You should know that. Remember how you chased after Mum until she finally gave in? Yes, I thought you might.'

'That's not the same at all,' he said. 'I loved your mother.'

She stopped walking to look at her father. 'What if I told you I was in love with Luiz?'

He looked at her for a long moment. Then he threw back his head and laughed so hard his eyes watered. He brushed the moisture away with the back of his hand, still chuckling but with a cynical tone to it that made her stomach feel uneasy. 'Did he say he was in love with you?'

'No, but I think he's coming round to—'

'He's looking out for himself, that's what he's doing,' he said. 'And I'm not referring to his big sponsorship deal everyone is talking about.'

Daisy didn't care for the snide expression on her father's face. Suspicion began to chill her blood until every hair on her head pulled away from her scalp. 'What do you mean?'

'I told him what I'd do with him if he didn't do the right thing by you.'

Something heavy lurched in her belly. 'You...you *threatened* him?'

'Not much, just enough to make sure he toed the line. I wasn't going to stand by and watch him trash my little girl's reputation with a one-night stand. He knew which side his bread was buttered. I made sure he ate it.'

Daisy couldn't believe it. Didn't want to believe it. The whole time Luiz had been with her he had been acting out of fear of her father? Had none of it meant anything to him—not one kiss, not one caress, not one passionate interlude—except as a way to save his own back? The man she had thought so gallant and kind was acting out of cowardice? How could it be true? It couldn't be true. He had been so convincing. She had fallen so hard and so fast. Was she really *that* naïve?

'I don't believe it. He wanted to be with me. I *know* he did. He wanted me to stay longer. He asked me to but I said no because—'

'He won't see you again,' her father said. 'He'll have someone else in his bed by now. You mark my words. Before you know it, someone will post a photo of him on social media with a new lover on his arm.'

Daisy didn't want her father to be right. It was too painful to think of Luiz replacing her before her plane had got off the ground. But what else was she to think? He had only been with her because of the pressure her father had put on him. It tarnished everything they had shared. Every moment they'd had together was tainted. Spoiled by the machinations of her father, who wanted to control every aspect of her life. His constant need to control her had ruined her one chance at finding happiness.

She had connected with Luiz. Not just physically, but emotionally. And it had happened right from that first breakfast. She had *seen* him. The *real* him. Without the mask he wore for everyone else. How could that have been an act on his part? Why would he let her in like that if he was only pretending to enjoy her company?

She had fallen in love with him. He had come to her rescue and kept her safe. Every time he had smiled at her she had fallen a little harder. Every time he touched her, kissed her or made love to her she had given him another piece of her heart. She had denied it to herself, not wanting to admit how much he had affected her. But he was everything she was looking for in a partner because without him she felt only half alive.

But he hadn't been with her for *her*.

He had been pretending the whole time. Acting his way through their four days together like an actor did a role he'd been assigned. Had *any* of their time together been real or was it all one big fake? What about that morning? Why had he asked her to stay? That surely couldn't have been because of what her father had said?

Daisy felt as if a blade had carved right through her heart, leaving it in shredded pieces hanging from her ribcage. Why couldn't he have flown with her back to England if he'd wanted more time with her? Surely he could have postponed his trip back to Argentina by a couple of days.

No. He would never do that because she was meant to fit into his life as if she had no life of her own. Just like her mother had been expected to fit into her father's life. To be what he wanted, when he wanted, where he wanted.

To be controlled.

'Come on,' her father said as he shepherded her towards the exit. 'I've got a special dinner planned. You know that new accountant I put on a few months ago? I'd like you to spend some time with him. I'm thinking of making him a partner. He can take over the business once I retire. He's exactly the sort of man I want as a son-in-law.'

Daisy stopped in her tracks and shook off her father's hold. 'What?'

'I don't think he'll be put off by your little fling in Vegas—' her father carried on as if she hadn't spoken '—he's probably sown a few wild oats himself. If I offer him a partnership to sweeten the—'

'Stop it right there,' she said through clenched teeth. 'I do *not* need you to organise my life for me. I do not need you to find me a husband or bribe someone to have dinner with me or anything else. How can you be so… so ridiculously obsessive about controlling everything I do? I'm not a kid any more. I'm an adult, Dad. I want to be in control of my own life. When are you going to finally accept that?'

Her father frowned as people glanced at them on their way past. 'Don't make a scene. You're acting like your mother, getting hysterical over nothing. I'm just trying to help you because I love you.'

'Do you?' Daisy asked. 'Do you really? You said you loved Mum but you never let her be herself. If you love me so much then why aren't I good enough the way I am?'

Her father's frown was dark and forbidding. 'What's got into you? Have you been eating too much sugar or something? You know how it makes you tetchy.'

Daisy repositioned her handbag strap over her shoulder. 'Maybe I've finally grown up.'

'You're letting one silly little fling go to your head,' he said. 'You'll forget about him soon enough. Once you meet Laurence you'll see what I mean. He's perfect for you. He reminds me of myself at that age.'

Great. Just what she needed. Another control freak in her life, hand-picked by her father.

Daisy kept walking towards the exit. 'Make my apologies. I have other plans.'

'You're jet-lagged. You always get irrational when you're over-tired. I can make it next week. How about that?'

She rolled her eyes as she faced him again. 'Dad. Read my lips. Stop controlling me.'

'A coffee?'

'No.'

He sucked in his lips and then pushed them out on a sigh, giving her the little boy lost look that normally would have seen her cave in. 'Does this mean you'll be moving out of the flat?'

Daisy gave him a determined look. 'I think it's time, don't you?'

Luiz stood a few metres away from the school gate, where an assortment of mothers and fathers and nannies or au pairs were collecting children. The icy wind was boring holes in his chest and making his eyes sting but he barely noticed. He had flown in that day after a week of playing charity matches in towns throughout Argentina. He had sent Daisy a few texts over the last few days but her replies had been distant and impersonal. He could hardly blame her, given how clumsily he had handled their parting back in Vegas. He hadn't had enough time to prepare for her leaving. He'd put it to the back of his mind, not wanting to face the fact their relationship would be on hold until he could free up some time to be with her. Offering to cover her wages… He still kicked himself over that. Of course she would be offended. Could he have thought of a worse way to insult her?

But he had a surprise for her that would make up for it. It had taken him this time apart to realise she was the only woman he could ever love. Perhaps a part of him had known it right from the start. Wasn't that why he had relaxed his guard? He had told her of his deepest hurts and she had listened with that gentle look on her face that made him feel as if a soothing balm had been spread over his raw wounds, finally giving them a chance to heal.

The last of the children were collected and the wind got icier as sleet started to fall. And then he saw her. She was dressed in a smart wool dress with a cashmere coat over the top and knee-high boots. A scarf was wound around her neck and her hair was in a tidy chignon at the back of her head. She had her head down against the wind-driven sleet but she must have sensed she was being watched for she suddenly glanced his way. Her eyes blinked and she touched the scarf at her throat with a nervous flutter of her hand. But then she gripped the strap of her bag a little tighter and stalked out of the school gates and towards the tube station a couple of blocks away.

He caught her before she got to the last wrought iron post of the school fence. 'Daisy. Wait.'

She swung around to face him, her cheeks rosy-red and her blue eyes flashing. 'I have nothing to say to you. I think my father said it all, don't you?'

He frowned. 'What has your father got to do with anything?'

She stood staunchly before him. 'Why don't you tell me?'

He took in her tightly set mouth and glittering eyes. 'I'm here because I need to talk to you.'

'I think you should find someone else to help you butter up your sponsors,' she said. 'I'm no longer available.'

A sharp pain seized him in the chest but there was no way he was going to let her see how much her cold statement hurt him. 'That didn't take you long. How long's it been? A week?'

She raised her chin. 'I'm sure you've filled my position seven times over.'

'Is that what you think?'

'It's what I expect from someone like you.'

Luiz drew in a breath and slowly released it. 'Right, well, then. I guess I should cancel my arrangements for the weekend.'

She glared at him. 'How *could* you?'

'How could I what?'

'Sleep with me because of what my father said.'

'Hang on a minute. I did not sleep with you because of anything your father said. I slept with you because I couldn't help myself.'

She threw him a scornful look. 'You expect me to believe that?'

'It's true,' Luiz said. 'I wanted you from the moment I laid eyes on you. Your father had nothing to do with it.'

Her forehead crinkled in an even deeper frown. 'But he told me he threatened you.'

'He did but I didn't take it seriously. Well, only a bit. But it didn't stop me from wanting you. I don't think any threat could do that.'

She chewed her lip for a moment. 'Why are you here?'

'We had an agreement, remember?'

She moved her gaze to look at a point in the distance, both of her hands gripping her bag strap so tightly he could see the small white bulges of her knuckles. 'I'm not sure I can go through with it… Not now…'

'Why not?'

She shifted her weight on the cobblestones and met his eyes. 'I think it's unwise to extend a holiday fling.'

'Why?'

'Because people aren't the same when they're back in their real worlds.'

'I came all this way to see you, *querida*,' he said. 'I've booked a luxury hotel. I've got a helicopter on standby to take you there. We can have the weekend together and shut out the rest of the world. Come on. What do you say?'

Her eyes hardened as they held his. 'Did you think to *ask* me if I'd like to be whisked away to a hotel for the weekend? What if I had other plans? What if I had already made my own arrangements?'

'You can cancel them, can't you?'

She blew out a whooshing breath. 'You're unbelievable. You think you can do anything you like by waving a fistful of money around. You're exactly like my father. You think you can control people by dangling big carrots under their nose. Well, you can find someone else to have your weekend with. I'm sure you won't have too much trouble. I'm not available, nor am I interested.'

Luiz stopped her spinning away by grabbing her arm. 'Wait a damn minute. I've rearranged my whole schedule to get here. I forfeited a training session with my team. That's a big deal so close to the Grand Slam.'

She looked at him with a steely glare. 'Why are you here, Luiz? Why are you *really* here?'

He thought about telling her but how could he do it like this? Not out on a cold and gloomy rain-sodden street with people looking on. He wanted to take her away and romance her, to show her just how much he loved her by treating her like a princess. 'I told you. I wanted to see you. We agreed to see each other for the next—'

'So you've seen me. Now you can go.'

His heart jerked with a spasm of pain so sharp it felt like someone had ripped it out of his chest. Disappointment chugged through him, making his legs feel numb and useless.

He'd been wrong.

Stupidly, gullibly wrong.

She didn't feel anything for him. She couldn't have made it clearer.

The blood was pounding in his head and his ears to a repetitive and sickening beat: *It. Is. Over. It. Is. Over.*

He let his hold fall away from her arm. 'Fine. If that's the way you want to play it. We'll leave it there.' He stepped back from her. '*Adios, querida.*'

She stood with soldier-straight shoulders, her lips barely moving as she said, 'Goodbye.'

* * *

Belinda scrolled through her Twitter feed. 'Nope. Not a thing about him anywhere. He hasn't posted anything since he was playing those charity matches in Argentina.' She put her phone down and gave Daisy a pointed look. 'Makes you kind of wonder, doesn't it?'

Daisy flattened her lips. 'He's probably too busy seducing some skinny supermodel.'

'Maybe.' Belinda leaned forward. 'Are you going to eat that cheesecake or just scowl at it?'

She shoved the plate in Belinda's direction. 'You have it.'

Belinda took a mouthful and then swallowed it before saying, 'Turning your nose up at cheesecake is a bad sign.'

'I'm not hungry.'

'Boy, you have got it bad, haven't you? I've never seen you like this before.'

Daisy dropped her head into her hands and squeezed bunches of her hair until her scalp stung. 'I'm so stupid. What was I thinking? A holiday fling with a career playboy? *Me?* God, what a pathetic joke.'

Belinda downed another mouthful of raspberry cheesecake. 'What exactly did your father say to him?'

'Does it matter?' Daisy sat back and folded her arms crossly. 'He expected me to drop everything and go with him. What planet is he from? I have a career. I have commitments. I have responsibilities I take very seriously. What does *he* do? He flies around the globe to sit on a horse and whack a ball with a mallet.'

Belinda scooped up a dollop of cream. 'He raised a lot of money for homeless kids in Argentina.'

'So?'

'Come on, Daze. You've got to admit that's pretty decent of him.'

Daisy let out a long breath. 'I wish he'd asked me first, you know? I mean, what sort of guy just *assumes* you've got nothing better to do than to wait for him to call?'

Belinda licked some raspberry coulis off the end of her fork. 'A guy in love doesn't always think. They act first.'

Daisy frowned. 'What do you mean?'

'Think about it. On the spur of the moment he asked you to stay with him a little longer but you declined. Then he flew to London after organising a surprise weekend getaway for you, which you also declined. Which, by the way, must have cost him a bomb. My guess is he's not going to ask again.'

'He didn't ask.' Daisy scowled. 'He *told* me.'

Belinda dug into the cheesecake again. 'Maybe you should ask him this time.'

'Ask him what?'

Belinda gave her a level look. 'If he's not in love with you, then why hasn't he been seen with anyone since?'

Luiz went through his warm-up routine in the changing room but his heart wasn't in it. His head wasn't in the right space. He couldn't concentrate. He couldn't think of anything but of how angry Daisy had been. How she had looked at him with such icy coldness. How she had frozen him out when all he had wanted was to whisk her away to tell her how he felt. He'd pinned so much on that trip. He had organised it down to the finest detail. Roses, champagne, gourmet food—everything a girl with her heart set on romance would want. How had he got it so wrong about her? Had he been so blindsided by his feelings he hadn't seen what was right under his nose?

She hadn't wanted *him*. Not the real him. She'd wanted a fling, an experience to look back on, just like all the other women who trailed after him.

It infuriated him to think that all those chatty little exchanges to get him to reveal his innermost secrets had been a ruse. She'd probably been laughing at him the whole time. She'd had no intention of continuing their affair. Not with her posh school board turning their noses up at her choice of partner. She probably had some stuck-up merchant banker by now. Someone her father approved of.

His gut twisted at the thought of her in another man's arms. It sickened him to think of another man kissing her. Touching her. Marrying her. Having babies with her.

He spun away and raked his head with his fingers. He had to stop thinking about her. It was over. He had to accept it. He thumped his fist on the lockers as if it would drum it into his skull. He. Had. To. Accept. It.

The crowds were milling into the stands. Alejandro and Teddy were being entertained in the sponsors' corporate marquee while he prepared for the game. The game he had spent years of his life training for; the game he was expected to win. The trophy was as good as his if he could just force himself to get out there and do what needed to be done.

He swore as he kicked his boot against the bench seat. What was the point of playing when the one person he was playing for wasn't here? Wasn't this for Daisy? Everything he had worked for he now wanted for her. She had shown him the shallowness of his life. His endless pursuit of pleasure without strings had all but strangled everything that was good in him.

Could he be wrong about her motives? Hadn't she made him see how much richer life could be when you lived it for others? Like she did. Devoting her life to the education of children. Sacrificing what she wanted so they could have what they needed. So different from his mother, who hadn't bothered to sacrifice anything for anyone.

Was he foolish to think he could try again with her? That this time he could ask her—*beg her*—to see him instead of assuming she would drop everything? She was proud and defiant. Hadn't he loved that about her from the moment he'd met her? She wasn't a pushover. She wasn't yet another sycophant. She was a genuine girl with a big heart who wanted the fairy tale. A fairy tale she deserved.

She had spent most of her life being controlled by her father. Why hadn't he realised his approach was exactly the same? He hadn't given her a choice. He had told her what he wanted as if she had no say in the matter. Of course she would cut him loose. Why would she sign up for more of the bulldozing tactics of her overbearing father?

Alejandro suddenly appeared in the doorway. 'There's someone here to see you.'

Luiz turned his back as he leaned his hands on the washbasin. He couldn't give a press interview now. Not now. Not while his emotions were so churned up inside his chest he couldn't breathe without it hurting. 'Tell them to go away.'

'I'm not sure she'll appreciate being told what to do.'

She?

His heart skipped a beat as he whipped back around. 'Who is it?'

'It's me,' Daisy said, stepping forward.

Luiz stared at her. He opened his mouth to speak but he couldn't get his vocal cords to respond. They were jammed by emotion so thick it paralysed his throat.

She was here?

He blinked to make sure he wasn't imagining her standing there. Like all those times as a kid, pressing his nose to the glass as he waited for his mother, only to have his heart plummet in disappointment when she didn't show up.

His mouth was dry. His heart was pounding so hard he could feel the echo of it beating in his fingertips.

'Aren't you going to say something?' Daisy said.

'Hello.' *Hello? Is that the best you could do?*

'I liked it when you said it in Argentinian.'

Luiz cleared his throat. '*Hola*.'

'I really like your brother.'

'He's married.'

'I know. I like his wife too. She's awfully sweet. You didn't tell me she was Theodora Marlstone, the brilliantly talented children's book illustrator. I've got all of her books. I use them in my class. My kids love them.'

Luiz swallowed again. Best not to get too ahead of himself. He wasn't going to let her rip his heart out again. 'Why are you here?'

'Why do you think I'm here?'

He searched her expression but she was playing him at his own game. He thought he was good at a poker face but she took it to a whole new level. 'I have no idea.'

For the first time a tiny crack appeared in her composure. 'Really? No idea at all?'

'You wanted to see a polo game?'

She let out a little breath. 'I guess you're still angry.'

'What gives you that idea?'

She chewed at her lip. 'You're not making this easy for me…'

'Did my brother set this up?'

'No. I came because I wanted to see you.'

'Why?'

Her blue eyes meshed with his. 'I wanted to ask you something.'

'Ask.'

She pressed her lips together for a moment, her gaze lowering slightly. 'Do you love me?'

Luiz watched the way her throat tightened, just as his had earlier. He watched as her teeth tugged at the inside of her mouth as if trying to control the urge to cry. His heart swelled in his chest until he could feel it pushing against his lungs. 'Yes.'

Her eyes flew back to his. '*Yes?*'

He smiled and closed the gap between them, reaching for her and hugging her close to his chest. 'Yes, you little goose. How could you think I didn't?'

'But my father—'

'Was right to warn me to keep my hands off his little princess, but do you think I could do it?' He cupped her face in his hands. 'I fell in love with you that first night. You put your nose in the air and gave me such a haughty look I was instantly smitten.'

'*Really?* That early on?'

He laughed as relief and joy spread through him. 'Of course it only made it worse when you did that stripper routine. What hope did I have after that?'

Her cheeks flushed in the way he adored so much. 'I think I fell in love with you when you came to my rescue. I didn't want to admit it, but when you stayed up all night watching over me I saw you in a completely different light. Of course, the way you kept plying me with delicious food only made it worse.'

He stroked her face. 'I'm sorry for how I handled things back in Vegas. It was such a crass offer. Not one of my proudest moments, that's for sure. I wanted you to stay but I didn't think of how you would take it. I stupidly assumed you'd jump at the chance. I should've known you'd do the opposite.'

She looked at him earnestly. 'It wasn't that I didn't want to be with you. I did. So much. But I couldn't bear to be just another one of your girls. I wanted to be special.'

He held her by the upper arms. 'You are, *mi amor.* So special I can barely find the words. I love you. I want to spend the rest of my life with you. Say you'll marry me.'

She gave him a teasing smile. 'Are you asking me or telling me?'

He grinned back. 'I'm begging you.'

'Well, that's different.'

'Is that a yes?'

Daisy linked her arms around his neck. 'How could I ever say no to you?'

He kissed her for a long breathless minute before pulling back to look at her glowing face and sparkling eyes. 'So, you've come all this way to see a polo game. I guess I'd better go out there and get that trophy.'

She gave him a look of mock reproach. 'Aren't you being terribly arrogant to assume you're going to win?'

He pressed another kiss to her lips. 'It would be if I was playing for myself.'

Daisy stood next to Teddy and Alejandro in the stands as Luiz came round for a victory lap after the thrilling game. He held the trophy high above his head as he sought her gaze in the stand, his dark eyes glinting as he mouthed the words, 'This one's for you, *querida*.'

Mills & Boon® Hardback

November 2014

ROMANCE

A Virgin for His Prize	Lucy Monroe
The Valquez Seduction	Melanie Milburne
Protecting the Desert Princess	Carol Marinelli
One Night with Morelli	Kim Lawrence
To Defy a Sheikh	Maisey Yates
The Russian's Acquisition	Dani Collins
The True King of Dahaar	Tara Pammi
Rebel's Bargain	Annie West
The Million-Dollar Question	Kimberly Lang
Enemies with Benefits	Louisa George
Man vs. Socialite	Charlotte Phillips
Fired by Her Fling	Christy McKellen
The Twelve Dates of Christmas	Susan Meier
At the Chateau for Christmas	Rebecca Winters
A Very Special Holiday Gift	Barbara Hannay
A New Year Marriage Proposal	Kate Hardy
A Little Christmas Magic	Alison Roberts
Christmas with the Maverick Millionaire	Scarlet Wilson

MEDICAL

Playing the Playboy's Sweetheart	Carol Marinelli
Unwrapping Her Italian Doc	Carol Marinelli
A Doctor by Day...	Emily Forbes
Tamed by the Renegade	Emily Forbes

1014GEN STD HB

ROMANCE

Christakis's Rebellious Wife	Lynne Graham
At No Man's Command	Melanie Milburne
Carrying the Sheikh's Heir	Lynn Raye Harris
Bound by the Italian's Contract	Janette Kenny
Dante's Unexpected Legacy	Catherine George
A Deal with Demakis	Tara Pammi
The Ultimate Playboy	Maya Blake
Her Irresistible Protector	Michelle Douglas
The Maverick Millionaire	Alison Roberts
The Return of the Rebel	Jennifer Faye
The Tycoon and the Wedding Planner	Kandy Shepherd

HISTORICAL

A Lady of Notoriety	Diane Gaston
The Scarlet Gown	Sarah Mallory
Safe in the Earl's Arms	Liz Tyner
Betrayed, Betrothed and Bedded	Juliet Landon
Castle of the Wolf	Margaret Moore

MEDICAL

200 Harley Street: The Proud Italian	Alison Roberts
200 Harley Street: American Surgeon in London	Lynne Marshall
A Mother's Secret	Scarlet Wilson
Return of Dr Maguire	Judy Campbell
Saving His Little Miracle	Jennifer Taylor
Heatherdale's Shy Nurse	Abigail Gordon

1014 GEN STD LP

Mills & Boon® Hardback

December 2014

ROMANCE

Taken Over by the Billionaire	Miranda Lee
Christmas in Da Conti's Bed	Sharon Kendrick
His for Revenge	Caitlin Crews
A Rule Worth Breaking	Maggie Cox
What The Greek Wants Most	Maya Blake
The Magnate's Manifesto	Jennifer Hayward
To Claim His Heir by Christmas	Victoria Parker
Heiress's Defiance	Lynn Raye Harris
Nine Month Countdown	Leah Ashton
Bridesmaid with Attitude	Christy McKellen
An Offer She Can't Refuse	Shoma Narayanan
Breaking the Boss's Rules	Nina Milne
Snowbound Surprise for the Billionaire	Michelle Douglas
Christmas Where They Belong	Marion Lennox
Meet Me Under the Mistletoe	Cara Colter
A Diamond in Her Stocking	Kandy Shepherd
Falling for Dr December	Susanne Hampton
Snowbound with the Surgeon	Annie Claydon

MEDICAL

Midwife's Christmas Proposal	Fiona McArthur
Midwife's Mistletoe Baby	Fiona McArthur
A Baby on Her Christmas List	Louisa George
A Family This Christmas	Sue MacKay

ROMANCE

Zarif's Convenient Queen	Lynne Graham
Uncovering Her Nine Month Secret	Jennie Lucas
His Forbidden Diamond	Susan Stephens
Undone by the Sultan's Touch	Caitlin Crews
The Argentinian's Demand	Cathy Williams
Taming the Notorious Sicilian	Michelle Smart
The Ultimate Seduction	Dani Collins
The Rebel and the Heiress	Michelle Douglas
Not Just a Convenient Marriage	Lucy Gordon
A Groom Worth Waiting For	Sophie Pembroke
Crown Prince, Pregnant Bride	Kate Hardy

HISTORICAL

Beguiled by Her Betrayer	Louise Allen
The Rake's Ruined Lady	Mary Brendan
The Viscount's Frozen Heart	Elizabeth Beacon
Mary and the Marquis	Janice Preston
Templar Knight, Forbidden Bride	Lynna Banning

MEDICAL

200 Harley Street: The Soldier Prince	Kate Hardy
200 Harley Street: The Enigmatic Surgeon	Annie Claydon
A Father for Her Baby	Sue MacKay
The Midwife's Son	Sue MacKay
Back in Her Husband's Arms	Susanne Hampton
Wedding at Sunday Creek	Leah Martyn

1114 GEN STD LP